The first shot went high and wild.

Clint didn't move. He couldn't show any fear, or concern.

"Wow," he called, "which of you fired that shot? That was way off. You must've rushed it."

No answer.

"Come on, boys, step out," he said. "Let's do this."

Tony Black stepped out of hiding. He was off to Clint's right.

"Where's Andy, Tony?"

"Here!"

He looked to his left. Andy stepped out, but he wasn't alone. He had Jason right in front of him.

Damn.

Clint stepped away from the house. He heard Stephanie out the front door, so he moved farther away. Now was out in the open, the center of a triangle formed by other three.

Okay, this was the situation he'd foreseen himself getting into—but not with Jason in the play.

"Okay," Stephanie said to him, "you wanted me to go my gun. Let's do it."

DON'T MISS THESE
ALL-ACTION WESTERN SERIES
FROM THE BERKLEY PUBLISHING GROUP

THE GUNSMITH by J. R. Roberts
Clint Adams was a legend among lawmen, outlaws, and
ladies. They called him . . . the Gunsmith.

LONGARM by Tabor Evans
The popular long-running series about Deputy U.S. Marshal
Custis Long—his life, his loves, his fight for justice.

SLOCUM by Jake Logan
Today's longest-running action Western. John Slocum rides
a deadly trail of hot blood and cold steel.

BUSHWHACKERS by B. J. Lanagan
An action-packed series by the creators of Longarm. The
rousing adventures of the most brutal gang of cutthroats ever
assembled—Quantrill's Raiders.

DIAMONDBACK by Guy Brewer
Dex Yancey is Diamondback, a Southern gentleman turned
con man when his brother cheats him out of the family for-
tune. Ladies love him. Gamblers hate him. But nobody pulls
one over on Dex . . .

WILDGUN by Jack Hanson
The blazing adventures of mountain man Will Barlow—from
the creators of Longarm!

TEXAS TRACKER by Tom Calhoun
J.T. Law: the most relentless—and dangerous—manhunter
in all Texas. Where sheriffs and posses fail, he's the best man
to bring in the most vicious outlaws—for a price.

THE GUNSMITH

390

COPPER CANYON KILLERS

J. R. ROBERTS

JOVE BOOKS, NEW YORK

THE BERKLEY PUBLISHING GROUP
Published by the Penguin Group
Penguin Group (USA) LLC
375 Hudson Street, New York, New York 10014

USA • Canada • UK • Ireland • Australia • New Zealand • India • South Africa • China

penguin.com

A Penguin Random House Company

COPPER CANYON KILLERS

A Jove Book / published by arrangement with the author

Copyright © 2014 by Robert J. Randisi.
Penguin supports copyright. Copyright fuels creativity, encourages diverse voices,
promotes free speech, and creates a vibrant culture. Thank you for having an authorized
edition of this book and for complying with copyright laws by not reproducing, scanning,
or distributing any part of it in any form without permission. You are supporting writers
and allowing Penguin to continue to publish books for every reader.

JOVE® is a registered trademark of Penguin Group (USA) LLC.
The "J" design is a trademark of Penguin Group (USA) LLC.

For information, address: The Berkley Publishing Group,
a division of Penguin Group (USA),
375 Hudson Street, New York, New York 10014.

ISBN: 978-0-515-15447-4

PUBLISHING HISTORY
Jove mass-market edition / June 2014

PRINTED IN THE UNITED STATES OF AMERICA

10 9 8 7 6 5 4 3 2 1

Cover illustration by Sergio Giovine.

This is a work of fiction. Names, characters, places, and incidents either are the product
of the author's imagination or are used fictitiously, and any resemblance to actual persons,
living or dead, business establishments, events, or locales is entirely coincidental.

If you purchased this book without a cover, you should be aware that this book is
stolen property. It was reported as "unsold and destroyed" to the publisher, and neither
the author nor the publisher has received any payment for this "stripped book."

ONE

Daniel Thayer rolled over in bed and gazed at the woman lying next to him. She was a long, lean blonde with beautifully shaped, small, pink-tipped breasts and long, lovely legs. On the bedpost behind them was a gun and holster, within easy reach.

They had just spent an energetic half hour pleasing each other, and were both trying to catch their breath.

"So," Thayer said, "you know what it is I want done?"

"I know," Stephanie Kitten said.

"And you can do it?"

She smiled, wiped some sweat from her upper lip with a thumb, then licked it off.

"Oh, I can do it," she said. "I can do lots of things."

"Well, I know that," Thayer said. He stood up, grabbed a blue silk robe from a nearby chair, slipped it on, and belted it. He was a man in his fifties, who kept himself in good physical shape.

Stephanie was in her thirties, a woman full of confi-

dence in her appearance and her abilities. The two had a
business relationship and—despite the fact that they had
sex from time to time—no personal relationship. The sex
was actually a way they had of sealing whatever deal they
happened to be making at the time.

He strolled over to a sideboard and poured himself a
glass of brandy. He did not offer Stephanie a glass.

The blonde reclined on the bed, one knee bent, allowing the air to dry the perspiration that dappled her beautiful body. Later, when she returned to her own room, she'd
have a slow, luxurious bath. She actually liked her sex the
way she liked her baths, but she never got that from Thayer.
He liked it quick—maybe that was because he simply
couldn't last very long. He was a virile man who kept himself in shape, and could possibly go all night if he'd take
some direction from Stephanie, but she'd learned a long
time ago that this man didn't take direction from anyone.
He thought being rich made him right.

Well, as long as he paid her well, Stephanie was willing to tell him what he wanted to hear.

"I need this to be done soon," he told her.

She reached behind her to grip the bedpost, which
stretched her marvelous body out. Her pink nipples were
sharply distended, but Thayer was beyond being excited
now. He'd already had sex with her, and he was done for
the night.

"No problem," she told him. "It'll be done."

"Today?"

"Well," she said, "I have to go home and take a bath,
but . . . I believe it can be done today."

Thayer carried his brandy to a chest of drawers. He set
the glass down on it, opened the top drawer, and took out

a thick, brown envelope. He turned and tossed the envelope onto the bed.

"You want to count it?"

She reached for the envelope with one hand and held it, as if testing the weight.

"No need," she said. "You've never shortchanged me yet."

"All right, then," Thayer said. "I guess we're done here. I need to get some sleep."

"Of course."

She slid off the bed and reached for her clothes. Thayer picked up his brandy and watched her dress. She pulled on her jeans, buttoned her shirt, then sat on the bed and pulled on her boots. Lastly, she took the gun belt off the bedpost and strapped it on.

Actually, seeing her there wearing her gun, he did begin to get a little excited again.

She picked up the envelope full of money and tucked it into her back pocket, then grabbed her black hat and set it atop her blond hair, which hung past her shoulders.

"The job'll be done before tonight," she told him. "Guaranteed."

"Okay," he said. "If that's true, there'll be another envelope for you."

She smiled and said, "I'll look forward to it."

He raised his glass to her and said, "Until tonight."

Outside the Thayer's house, Stephanie ran into her two partners, who had been waiting there since she went inside.

"The old guy was quicker than usual tonight," Tony Black said with a grin.

"He's not so old, Tony," she said, "but yeah, he was quick."

"You get the money?" Andy Choate asked.

"First half," she said, showing them the envelope.

Tony Black was Stephanie's age, mid-thirties. In fact, they had grown up together, were almost like brother and sister as far as she was concerned. He wanted their relationship to be more, but she just couldn't see it. It would have been like incest, which she found disgusting. She knew some brothers and sisters who didn't mind having sex, but that wasn't the way she thought.

Andy Choate was like a slow cousin to them. He was younger, still in his late twenties, and did whatever they told him to do.

"So when do we do this?" Choate asked.

"Today," she said, "but first I need a bath, and some sleep."

"We all need some sleep," Black said. "Andy, go home and meet us for breakfast at the usual place."

"Okay," Andy said. "G'night."

As Andy walked away, Tony said to Stephanie, "I could use a bath myself."

She knew what he meant, but she said, "Fine, you can use the water after I'm finished. That's as close as you're gonna get."

TWO

When Clint Adams rode into Copper Canyon, Wyoming, he was a new man.

At least, he liked to think he was.

He had decided that in his future travels he was going to start minding his own business. Yes, he had decided it before, but this time he was determined to stick to his guns. Travel across the country, enjoy the food and the gambling and the women, and stay out of trouble. And if he did find trouble, it would be his own, not other people's.

It was actually his friend, Rick Hartman, who had talked him into this new mind-set when he had recently spent time in Labyrinth, Texas . . .

Sitting in Rick's Place, Hartman's saloon and gambling hall, Clint had shared a beer with his friend, and listened to his advice.

"You can't solve everybody's problems, Clint," Rick told him.

"I know that, Rick."

"Then why do you try?" Rick asked. "Every time you get a telegram from a friend in trouble, you run. And even when you're not asked, if you see somebody in trouble, you step in. You end up with people shooting at you."

"People shoot at me anyway."

"That's true," Rick said. "They shoot at you because you're the Gunsmith. But you don't have to become a target by presenting yourself front and center in their sights."

"That's not my aim."

"I know it," Rick said. "Look, how about trying it my way for a while? When you ride out of here, see if you can stay out of other people's troubles until you come back here. What'll that be? Weeks? Months?"

Clint frowned. Could he turn people down when they asked for his help? Especially friends?

"What do you say?" Rick asked. "Give it a try?"

Clint raised his mug and replied, "Why not?"

That had been several weeks ago. So far he'd been able to stick with it. He'd encountered a man who was losing his business in Northern Texas, and another man who was in danger of losing his ranch in Kansas, and he'd managed to stay out of it. He'd left town both times without looking back. And just a few days ago, after he'd ridden into Wyoming, he'd heard shots in the distance. At one time he would have ridden hard to see what was happening, but this time he ignored the shots and rode the other way.

It hadn't been easy, but he'd done it.

Now he rode into Copper Canyon, feeling that he was able to adhere to his agreement with Rick Hartman and stay out of trouble. He was just here to eat, maybe gamble, and see what kind of women the town had to offer.

* * *

Jason Henry entered the mercantile store with his list in his hand. This was the first time his father had trusted him to come to town and shop for supplies, and he wanted to get it right.

He walked in, and found the store empty. He looked around for Mr. Collins, the owner, but didn't see him or any customers. He found that odd. It was the middle of the day, and the store was usually busy, because Copper Canyon was a growing town.

"Mr. Collins?" he called.

No answer. He thought maybe the man might be in the storeroom. He'd never been back there, but his father had pointed it out to him once, telling him that a lot of the store's supplies were kept back there.

"Mr. Collins?" he asked, walking back to the storeroom doorway . . .

In the storeroom Tony Black pressed the barrel of his gun tightly into Ed Collins's spine and said, "Not a word."

"That's Jason Henry," Collins said. "The boy might come back here."

"If he does, he'll be sorry," Andy Choate said.

"Quiet!" Stephanie Kitten hissed.

All three men fell silent. Collins was sweating profusely. The sixty-eight-year-old merchant wasn't sure what the three people wanted, but he knew it wasn't good. They'd looked like trouble when they first entered the store, scaring away his customers, and when they produced their guns, he started to sweat.

"Mr. Collins!" the boy shouted from the store.

"If he comes in here," Stephanie whispered, "he's dead."

"Let me keep him out," Collins said.

Tony gripped the back of the merchant's neck so hard the man winced.

"You'll try to run," Tony said.

"I won't!" Collins said. "I just don't want the boy hurt."

Andy looked at Stephanie.

"Talk to him from the doorway," she told Collins.

"Steph—" Tony started, but she cut him off.

"Shut up!" She looked at Collins, gestured with her gun. "Go!"

Tony released his hold on Collins, who moved toward the doorway, pushed aside the curtain that covered it.

"Hey, Mr. Collins," Jason said, smiling broadly. "I was lookin' for ya—"

"Run, Jason!" Collins yelled. "Run!"

"Stupid!" Stephanie said. She grabbed Collins, pulled him back from the door, and struck him in the face with her gun. "Get the boy!" she yelled at Tony and Andy.

But they didn't have to chase Jason Henry. The seventeen-year-old stuck his head through the curtain, frowning, and said, "Mr. Collins."

Stephanie almost brought her gun down on the top of his head, but thought better of it. Instead, she grabbed him, wrapped her arm around his neck from the back, and choked him until he was unconscious.

"You killed him!" Collins said. He was down on one knee, holding his head.

"No," she said, taking her gun out again and pointing it at him, "he killed you."

THREE

Daniel Thayer sat behind his desk in his office.

When the new City Hall was built, he chose a back office on the second floor for himself. He had a window, but it overlooked the back alley. He didn't want the distraction of having the town right outside his window. He also couldn't hear what was going on out in front of the building. Unless there was a shoot-out right in front, he didn't think he would ever have heard a thing. If the bank was robbed, with shots fired, he'd have to be told about it. Similarly, if someone in town was shot to death, he wouldn't know until someone came to his office with the news.

After Clint had secured lodging for both himself and Eclipse, his Darley Arabian, he'd gone out in search of a steak. He'd found one that was pretty good, and now he was washing it down with a cold beer at Milty's Saloon.

That was where he was when he heard the shots.

The bartender's head jerked up at the sound of the first one. Chairs scraped the floors as patrons rose to their feet when the second shot sounded.

Clint's first instinct was to leave the bar and go to the door, but he managed to quell the urge and concentrate on his beer.

"You hear that?" the bartender asked.

"I did," Clint said.

"Ain't you curious?"

"The town's got law, right?"

"Yeah, Sheriff Brown, but—"

"Well, I'm sure he can handle it."

The bartender frowned.

"You are the Gunsmith, right?" he asked. "I recognized you when you came in."

"So?"

Still frowning, the bartender said, "You don't mind if I go out to see what happened, do you?"

"I've still got most of my beer," Clint said, raising his mug, "so I don't mind at all."

The bartender put down his bar rag, rushed around the bar and through the batwing doors. Some of the patrons had gone outside; others were just staring out the windows or over the batwing doors.

Clint smiled, and sipped his beer.

Sheriff Gordon Brown heard the shots and rushed out of his office. He didn't know where his deputy was. The young man was supposed to be making his rounds, and the sheriff hoped the worst hadn't happened.

A man was running by and Brown grabbed him.

"Where'd those shots come from?" he demanded.

"The mercantile," the man said. "At least, that's what somebody said."

When he let the man go, he took off running toward the mercantile. The sheriff followed him.

Clint was surprised when the girl sidled up alongside him at the bar. She wasn't a saloon girl. She was wearing jeans, a man's shirt, a worn jacket, and a battered hat.

"Ain't you curious?" she asked.

"About what?"

"The shots."

"When shots are fired," Clint said, "the smart thing to do is go the other way."

"But I heard Randy—the bartender—say you was the Gunsmith."

"That's right."

"Well . . . you don't run away from shots."

"What makes you say that?"

"Your reputation."

Clint leaned toward her. She was dirty, but beneath the dirt she was also pretty.

"You can't believe everything you hear," he told her.

"Mebbe not."

"What about you?" he asked.

"Whataya mean?"

"Aren't you curious?"

"I don't carry a gun," she said. "I don't go nowhere near shootin'."

"See," he said. "That's why you and I are still alive. We don't go near shooting."

"I guess." She closed one eye and regarded him critically. "Kinda disappointin', though."

"What is?"

"Findin' out that the Gunsmith don't go near shootin'."

"I'm sorry you're disappointed." Clint finished his beer.

"You want another one?" she asked.

"The bartender's not here."

"That don't matter," she said, moving around behind the bar. "I kin get it."

"Won't Randy get mad?"

"Naw," she said, drawing the beer. "He's my uncle. An' he lets me relieve him as bartender sometimes."

She set the full beer in front of him, with just the right amount of foam.

"Thanks."

"It's the mercantile," somebody yelled. "The shootin' happened at the mercantile."

The girl raised her eyebrows at Clint.

"Why would somebody shoot up the mercantile?" she asked.

"Robbery?"

"I'd rather rob the bank."

"Then maybe you should go over and find out," he said.

"Naw," she said, "Uncle Randy'll tell me when he comes back. You, too, if you're still here."

She drew herself a beer.

"Are you old enough for that?"

"I'm twenty-five," she said testily.

"Sorry," he said as she sipped her beer, "I couldn't tell under all that dirt."

FOUR

"All right, all right, everybody clear out!" Sheriff Brown shouted. "Come on, everybody out."

"It's Collins, Sheriff," somebody said. "That kid killed him."

"What kid?"

"Jason Henry."

"What?"

"Everybody knows that boy ain't right in the head," somebody else said. "Now he's gone and kilt poor Mr. Collins."

"Where's the body?" he asked. "Anybody?"

The crowd was filing out the door, but from the back room Brown's deputy, Kenny Ott, stepped through the curtain.

"Back here, Sheriff."

"Where have you been?" Brown asked.

"I was makin' my rounds, Sheriff," Ott said. "I heard the shots and came runnin'."

"And found what?"

"Ed Collins, on the floor, shot twice," the young deputy said. "And Jason Henry crouched over him."

"Where's Jason?"

"He's in the back," the deputy said.

"With the victim?"

"Don't worry," Ott said. "I tied him up."

"Did you arrest him?"

"Yes, sir."

"All right," Brown said, "take me to him."

"Right back here."

Jason Henry was sitting on the floor, his hands tied behind his back. His head was pounding, and his throat hurt. He was staring at Mr. Collins, who was lying on the floor. He was waiting for Mr. Collins to move.

Why wouldn't Mr. Collins move?

The sheriff entered the back room. First he saw Collins on the floor, obviously shot twice. Then he saw Jason Henry, sitting in a corner.

"Sheriff," Jason said. "Can I go home now?"

"Not quite yet, Jason," Brown said. "We need to have a talk."

Jason looked at Collins.

"Why won't Mr. Collins wake up?" he asked.

"Because he's dead, Jason," Sheriff Brown said. "Do you know what 'dead' means?"

"Y-Yeah," Jason said. "I know. It's like my m-ma. She's dead."

"That's right," Brown said. "Just like your ma." He

turned to Deputy Ott. "Kenny, take Jason over to the office, will you?"

"Yessir. Should I put him in a cell?"

"No," Brown said. "Just park him in a chair in front of my desk. I'll be there soon."

"Okay."

Ott helped Jason Henry get to his feet and walked him toward the door.

"And Kenny?"

"Yeah?"

"Pick four men out there and send them in," the sheriff said. "I want them to carry Mr. Collins over to the undertaker's office."

"Yes, sir."

"Sheriff," Jason said, "can I see my pa?"

"Sure, Jason," Brown said. "I'm gonna send for him right now. He'll be here soon. Now you go with Kenny and wait for me in my office."

"O-Okay."

Ott walked him out.

Gordon Brown leaned down over Ed Collins and examined the body. Two shots in the back. He looked around for a gun, didn't see one. Maybe Kenny had it and forgot to say so.

Or maybe there was no gun.

He stood up and searched the room, still didn't find any guns.

Four men appeared at the curtained doorway, struggling to get in together.

"You men," Sheriff Brown said, "carry poor Mr. Collins over to the undertaker's office."

"Yeah, okay, Sheriff," one of them said.

Brown watched as the four men lifted the body, each careful not to get blood on themselves. As the body came off the floor, he saw the gun.

Damn. If there had been no gun in the room, it would have been unlikely that Jason could have shot Collins. But with this gun—a Colt Peacemaker that had seen better days—present, he couldn't just assume Jason's innocence.

Fuck.

He picked up the gun, checked the loads. Two shots had been fired. He tucked the gun into his belt, then walked through the store and out. He pulled the door closed behind him. There was still a crowd in front of the store, and he recognized many of them.

"Is it true, Sheriff?" Randy the bartender asked. "Did Jason Henry kill Ed Collins?"

"We don't know anything yet, Randy," Brown said.

"But you arrested the boy," somebody said.

"We took Jason to my office to question him," Brown said. "That's all for now. Now I think you folks better get back to your business, or whatever you were doing. There's nothing to see here anymore."

Sheriff Brown walked away as the crowd began to disperse. He'd almost asked somebody to ride out to the Henry ranch to get Jason's father, Big Al Henry, but in the end he decided that was something he should probably do himself.

Of course, that was after he questioned Jason to find out what had happened.

FIVE

"I don't know," Jason Henry said.

"Come on, son," the sheriff said. "I'm trying to help you."

"I wanna go home," Jason said.

"Not yet," Brown said. "Tell me what happened. Why did you go to the store?"

"Pa said I could buy the supplies," Jason said. "He give me a list." He dug into his short pockets, came out with a folded piece of caper. The deputy took it and handed it to Sheriff Brown.

"Okay, so you were gonna buy supplies," Brown said. "You walked in and . . . what?"

"I didn't see Mr. Collins so I called him," Jason said. "He didn't answer, so I kept callin'."

"And?"

"I thought maybe he was in the back room. I ain't never been back there, and I didn't wanna get in trouble."

Jason stopped there, and Brown had to urge him further.

"Come on, Jason," he said. "Tell us the whole story. What happened next?"

"I went to the doorway and I put my head through the curtain," the boy said.

"And?"

"Somebody grabbed me and they choked me," Jason said, almost tearing up. "They hurt my throat."

"And what happened to Mr. Collins?"

"I don't know," Jason said. "I fell asleep, and when I woke up, Mr. Collins was on the floor."

"Did you touch Mr. Collins?"

"Well, yeah . . . shook him, tryin' to wake him up."

"And then?"

"And then he came in and pointed a gun at me," Jason said, pointing at the deputy. "He scared me. Then he tied me up. Did Mr. Collins wake up?"

"No," Sheriff Brown said, "I told you, Jason, Mr. Collins is dead."

Jason looked sad.

"Did you kill him?"

Now Jason looked surprised.

"Me? I didn't kill him, Sheriff!"

"Did you see anybody else, Jason?"

"No."

"No other customers in the store?"

"No."

"Did you hear anything?"

"I didn't hear nothin'," Jason said. "Somebody grabbed me and I . . . I went to sleep."

Brown sat back in his chair and studied the young man. He didn't think Jason had it in him to shoot anybody, but he wouldn't be doing his job if he just let him go home.

"Jason, did you have a gun with you?"

"No" Jason said. "My pa don't let me carry no gun."

The sheriff pointed to the gun on the desk in front of him. It was the gun he found beneath Collin's body.

"I found that gun on the floor. It's not yours?"

"No sir!"

"Well," Brown said, "it belongs to somebody, and you didn't see anybody else there."

"Maybe it was Mr. Collins's?"

"I don't know," Brown said.

"Sheriff," Jason said, "when can I go home?"

"Not yet, Jason," Brown said.

"Where's my pa?"

"Who did you come to town with?"

"I came on a buckboard with Terry Wilson, one of Pa's hands," Jason said.

"And where is he?"

"He said he'd be at the saloon."

"He must have heard the shots," Ott said. "So where is he?"

"I don't know," Jason said mournfully.

"Okay," Brown said, "Kenny, take Jason and put him in a cell."

"I'm goin' to jail?"

"Just for a while, Jason," Brown said. "While you're here, we'll go and find Terry Wilson."

"And my pa?"

Brown nodded.

"And your pa."

Deputy Ott took Jason by the arm and walked him back to the cell block. He put him into a cell, and the boy flinched when the door snapped closed.

"Deputy?"

"Yeah?"

"I'm hungry."

"Don't worry," Ott said. "We'll feed you."

When Ott came out, Sheriff Brown was staring down at the gun on his desk.

"What do we do now?" Ott asked.

"You find Terry Wilson," Brown said. "If he's not in any of the saloons, try the whorehouse. He might have lied to Jason about where he'd be."

"Right. What are you gonna do?"

"I'm going to ride out to the Henry ranch and tell Big Al that his son is in my jail."

Kenny Ott did not envy the sheriff his task. Big Al Henry was not going to be happy about his son being in jail.

Both men headed for the door, but before they reached it, it opened and a woman stepped in. She was young, pretty, and obviously very upset.

"Sheriff," the young woman said, "where is he?"

"Beth—"

"Where is the sonofabitch who killed my dad?" Beth Collins demanded.

SIX

Clint was finishing his second beer as people came filing back into the saloon. Randy the bartender took up his place behind the bar.

"Who gave you the second beer?" he asked.

"A girl who said she was your niece."

"Letty?"

"I don't know her name," Clint said. "She was kind of dirty, maybe pretty under all the dirt."

"That's Letty," Randy said. "I've told her to stay out from behind the bar."

"That's not what she said."

"No, she wouldn't," Randy said. "You curious about what happened out there?"

"I figure you're going to tell me," Clint said, "whether I'm curious or not."

"What makes you say that?"

"You're a bartender," Clint said. "That's what you do."

Other men lined up at the bar and Randy took the time to serve them some beers. They were talking among themselves about what had happened.

"Ed Collins, who owned and ran the mercantile, was shot and killed."

"I heard that much from the conversations around me," Clint said. "Who did it?"

"From what we heard," Randy said, "he was shot by Jason Henry."

"And?"

"Well, Jason's a kid, Big Al Henry's kid."

"Who's Al Henry?"

"Biggest rancher in the county."

"Ah."

Randy shook his head.

"I can't believe it."

"Why not?"

"Well, Jason's kind of . . . slow," Randy said. "He's a good kid, only about seventeen."

"So?"

"They found him with the body."

"Doesn't mean he did it."

"Well, he's in a cell," Randy said, "and the sheriff is gonna go get his father."

"Too bad," Clint said, "but I don't know any of these people."

"You want another beer?"

"Sure."

"I'm going to give you that second one on the house, because Letty gave it to you."

"I'll be sure to thank Letty."

"You stay away from my Letty," Randy said. "She's just a kid."

"She told me she's twenty-five."

Randy fixed Clint with a hard stare and said, "That's a kid in my book."

"Okay," Clint said. "You're the uncle."

"Damn right." He set the beer down in front of Clint so hard it sloshed onto the bar.

Sheriff Gordon Brown rode up to the main house at the Henry ranch, which was only about fifteen minutes outside of town. He dismounted and knocked on the door.

"Sheriff," Dan Robards said. He was the foreman of the ranch, a man in his forties who had been a hand for a long time before being promoted to his current job.

"Dan," Brown said, "I've got to see your boss."

"He's in his office," Robards said. "He don't like to be disturbed."

"Well, he'll have to be."

"It's important?"

"Real Important."

"Okay, then," Robards said. "Come on in." He let Brown enter and closed the door. "I'll get him. Wait here."

Brown waited by the door for five minutes before two men returned. Big Al Henry lived up to his name. He was maybe six-five, with broad shoulders, in his sixties, had not gone to fat but was thickening. His hair was pure white, rolled back from his forehead in waves.

"Sheriff," he said, "come on into the living room with me."

"Yes, sir."

"Something to drink?" Big Al asked. "Coffee? Whiskey?"

"Nothin', thanks."

The rancher turned to face the sheriff as they got into the living room, furnished with expensive, overstuffed furniture.

"It must be serious if you don't want a drink."

"It is," Brown said. "It's about Jason."

Big Al froze.

"What about him?"

"He's in my jail."

It wasn't unusual for Big Al to hear that one of his men was in jail, but not his son.

"He's seventeen."

"I know."

"And he's not all there."

"I know that, too."

"Why is he in your jail, Gordon?"

"Well . . . murder."

Big Al looked stunned, then said, "That's ridiculous. Who is he supposed to have killed?"

"Ed Collins."

"Collins. Oh damn, I sent him to the store. What did the kid walk into?"

"There were shots, and he was found crouching over Ed's body."

"Preposterous!" Big Al said.

"Well, he was the only one there. Collins was on the floor and there was a gun under him."

"Not in Jason's hand?"

"No."

"I think you've overstepped yourself, Sheriff."

"I'm doin' my job, Mr. Henry. Ed's daughter, Beth, is out for Jason's head. She's talking to the judge."

"Miller!" Henry said. He and Judge Miller were not friends. "He'll use this to crucify me."

"Al, Jason is asking for you."

"Yes, yes," Henry said, "I'll come at once. You ride ahead and tell the boy I'm coming."

"Sure, Al. Sure."

The foreman, Robards, was standing just outside the living room, his hands clasped in front of him.

"Dan, take him back to his horse, and then come back. And have my horse saddled."

"Yes, sir."

As Brown started to leave the room, Al Henry said, "Gordon."

"Yes?"

"What happened to the man we sent with Jason?" Henry looked at Robards. "Who went with him?"

"Terry Wilson."

"Oh, yeah, Wilson," Henry said. "What happened to him?"

"We're looking for him now."

"He's probably in the whorehouse," Robards said.

"All right," Big Al said to Brown, "I'll see you in town." Brown nodded, and left.

By the time Dan Robards returned, Big Al Henry had a cigar going. He was still standing in the center of the room, deep in thought.

"Your horse is bein' saddled," the foreman said.

"Good," Henry said. "saddle yours, too. You're coming with me."

"Okay."

"Not a word to the boy's mother, understand?" Henry said. "She's not to know about this."

"Sure, boss."

"And keep it from the hands, too, for now," Big Al said. "Otherwise she might get wind of it."

"Okay."

"That goddamned kid. I never should have sent him to town."

"It's not your fault, boss."

"No? Whose, then? Yours?"

"Mine?"

"For sending that idiot Wilson with him."

"He was supposed to keep an eye on him."

"That's what I mean," Henry said. "Oh, never mind whose fault it is. Get your horse saddled and meet me outside."

"Okay, boss."

"And Dan?"

"Yeah?"

"Wear a gun."

"Yes, sir."

SEVEN

Clint was standing outside the saloon when the sheriff came riding back to town. He watched as the man reined in his horse in front of his office and went inside. He hadn't checked in with the lawman yet, so he crossed the street and entered without knocking.

The sheriff turned quickly and stared at him.

"Sheriff?"

"That's right," the man said. "Sheriff Brown. What can I do for you?"

"Nothing, really," Clint said. "I rode into town today and thought I'd check in with you."

"And why would you do that?"

"My name is Clint Adams."

The sheriff looked surprised.

"The Gunsmith!"

"That's right."

"I hope you're not in town looking for trouble, Mr. Adams," Brown said. "I've got all I can handle right now."

"So I've heard," Clint said. "No, I'm just passing through, thought I'd try your beer and steaks . . . maybe some gambling."

"Well, you're welcome to it all," Brown said. "Like I said, I've got other problems."

"I won't keep you, then," Clint said.

At that point the deputy walked in.

"You find Wilson?"

"I did," Ott said. "He was at the whorehouse."

"Where is he now?"

"He's getting cleaned up," the deputy said. "Who's this?"

"Meet Clint Adams."

"The Gunsmith?"

"We've gone over that already," Brown said. "He's simply passing through—and he was just leaving."

"Yes, I was," Clint said.

He turned and walked out. He was tempted to stop and listen at the door, but reminded himself that this was none of his business.

He walked away, quite proud of himself.

"What the hell—" Brown said to Ott. "Where's Wilson?"

"I told you, he's gettin' cleaned up," Ott said. "I found him in a room with three girls."

"Three?"

"Three," Ott said. "They was all naked and kinda . . . messy."

"Okay," Brown said, "okay, I don't want to hear about it. Just go and get the kid something to eat." Brown gave the deputy a hard look. "He's still back there, isn't he?"

"Oh, he's there."

"Okay. Go to the café down the street."

"That place ain't very good, Sheriff."

"I didn't say get *us* something to eat, I said get *him* something to eat."

"Oh, okay. What should I get him?"

Brown thought a moment, then said, "Chicken. They can't ruin that."

"Yes, sir."

Ott left and Brown sat down behind his desk. He expected the boy's father any minute. He had a quick drink from a bottle in his drawer, then went into the cell block.

Jason got to his feet immediately and rushed to the bars.

"Am I going home now?" he asked hopefully.

"Not right now, Jason."

"Is my pa here?"

"Not yet, but he's on the way," Brown said. "I spoke with him myself."

"Did you find Terry?"

"Oh, yeah," Brown said. "We found him. He'll be here soon, too. Also, Deputy Ott is bringing you some chicken."

The boy brightened.

"I like chicken."

"Good. It'll be here shortly. Sit back down and wait. Okay?"

"Okay."

Jason went and sat back down on his cot.

Clint was sitting in a chair in front of his hotel when two men rode into town. One of them sat very tall in the saddle. They both reined in their horses in front of the jail.

The tall man dismounted, removed his hat, ran his hand over his white hair, and returned the hat to his head. Clint assumed this was the incarcerated boy's father.

But it didn't concern him.

Not at all.

"Where's my boy?" Big Al demanded.

"In a cell," the sheriff replied.

"Anybody else back there?"

"No," Brown said. "We're about to feed him."

"Never mind," Henry said. "I'll feed him myself, in a restaurant."

"Al—"

"I wanna see him."

"Go ahead."

Al Henry started for the cell blocks.

"I'll need you to leave your gun here, Mr. Henry," Brown said.

Big Al glared at the lawman, then took his gun from his holster and set it on the desk.

"Wait here," Al told his foreman.

"Yes, sir."

As Big Al went into the cell block, Brown asked Robards, "He's not gonna do anything stupid, is he?"

"Not that I know of," the foreman said. "But then, I don't know what goes on in his head. You've got his only son in jail for murder."

"Well," Brown said, "he hasn't been charged . . . yet."

EIGHT

As Clint watched, a young woman and an older man in a suit hurried down the street and went directly to the sheriff's office. They entered without knocking.

Still none of his business.

As the two people entered, both Sheriff Brown and Dan Robards turned to look.

"Beth!" Brown said.

"And Judge Miller," Robards said.

"Sheriff," Beth Collins said, "I brought the judge."

"I can see that."

"Brown, what the hell is going on?" Judge Miller asked.

"Didn't she tell you, Judge?"

"I'm asking you!"

"Well," Brown said, "it's like this . . ."

In the cell block Big Al saw his boy sitting in his jail cell and shook his head. If his mother could see him now.

"Jason."

"The boy looked up, saw his father, and leaped to his feet.

"Pa! You gettin' me outta here?"

"I am," Henry said, "but first I want to know what happened."

"I don't know, Pa," Jason said. "I saw Mr. Collins lyin' there and then . . . I don't know. Somebody choked me." He touched his neck. "They hurt my throat, and then I woke up. I thought Mr. Collins was asleep, but the sheriff says he's . . . dead . . . like Ma."

The boy's natural mother had died years ago, but Big Al's present wife, Nancy, has raised him from a pup, considered him to be hers.

"Son—" Big Al said, but then he heard the commotion out front. "I'll be right back."

He went back into the office and saw Judge Miller.

"What the hell do you want?" Big Al asked.

"I want to do my job, Al," Miller said. "From what the sheriff tells me, it sounds like your boy killed Ed Collins."

"That's nonsense!"

"My pa is dead, Mr. Henry!" Beth said. "Is that nonsense?"

"No, of course not, Miss Collins," Al Henry said, "but my boy . . . you know he couldn't have done that."

"I don't know any such thing," she said.

"Sheriff," Henry said, "I want my boy out of that cell now."

"Not a chance," Judge Miller said. "The boy's to be held over for trial."

"That's ridiculous."

"You can't be serious," Henry said. "There's no evidence."

"He was found in the room with the body, and a gun," Miller said.

"None of that means anything," Big Al Henry said.

"That'll be up to a jury."

The two men faced off. They were the same age, but Henry towered over the portly judge—still they both had a strong presence, like two immovable forces.

Big Al Henry looked over at the desk, where his gun was lying.

"Don't do anything stupid, Al," Sheriff Brown said.

"Don't worry," Henry said. He picked up his gun and holstered it. "When I do something, it won't be stupid."

The door opened then and the deputy walked in carrying a tray of food, covered by a red and white checkered napkin.

"Wow," he said, stopping short. To the judge, he explained, "Food for the prisoner."

"Give it to him," the judge said. "We don't want it to be said the prisoner was mistreated."

Ott looked at the sheriff, who nodded. The deputy carried the tray into the cell block.

"I'll check my docket and let you know when the trial is," Miller said to Brown. "You can then inform the others."

"Yessir."

"My dear," he said, taking Beth's elbow. They left together.

"You know why he's doing this, don't you?" Big Al asked the sheriff.

"What happened, Al?" Brown asked. "You guys used to be friends."

"That was a long, long time ago," Henry said. "Tell my boy I'll be back for him."

Big Al Henry stormed out of the office, with his foreman behind him.

Just outside the office, Big Al ran into Terry Wilson. The rancher didn't recognize him until Robards said something.

"Terry!" the foreman said. "What the hell—"

"Wilson?" Al Henry said.

"Yessir," Wilson said nervously.

"Where the hell have you been?" Robards asked.

"Never mind that," Al Henry said. "Where the hell were you when my boy was gettin' into trouble?"

"I'm sorry, sir," Wilson said, "I thought he'd be all right while I, uh—"

"While you went and rutted with your whores?" Big Al demanded.

"Well, sir—"

"It was your job to keep him out of trouble."

"I know, sir," Wilson said. "I'm sor—"

"Never mind," Henry said. "You better go in and talk to the sheriff, then when you get back to the ranch, draw your pay."

"What?"

"You're fired!"

"But—"

Big Al ignored the man and walked away.

"But—" Wilson tried with the foreman, but Robards also ignored him and walked to his horse.

Glumly, Terry Wilson turned and walked into the sheriff's office.

NINE

Clint watched—not with great interest, but some—as people stormed out of the sheriff's office. The pretty young woman—from across the street she looked about twenty or so—was almost dragged up the street by the man in the suit, who had a definite air of self-importance.

A few minutes after that, the tall, white-haired man burst out the door, with the other man trailing behind him. They ran into a third man, who they both seemed to light into. Then they got on their horses. But didn't go far. They stopped in front of the saloon Clint had been in when the shooting happened. They dismounted and went inside, in an obvious drinking mood.

The third man went into the sheriff's office.

Clint could have walked over to the saloon out of curiosity, just to see if the two men were talking about what went on in the sheriff's office, but he decided against it. After all, it was none of his business.

Instead, he stood up and decided to go in search of a place to have supper.

"What's that?" Big Al Henry said, looking at the bartender. He hadn't been listening to the man, but something he'd said had penetrated. "What did you say?"

"Oh, I was just sayin' that Clint Adams, the Gunsmith, was in town," Randy replied.

"What's he doing here?"

"Just passin' through."

"What was he doing in this saloon?"

"He was just havin' a few beers."

"He's a killer," Henry said. "Maybe he killed Ed Collins."

"Couldn't've, Mr. Henry," Randy said.

"Why not?"

"Because he was right here, standin' where you are, when we heard the shots."

"Did he go over to see what happened?"

"No, sir," Randy said. "He stayed right here."

"While everybody else was runnin' out to see what happened?" Henry asked. "Why?"

Randy shrugged and said, "He told me it waren't none of his business."

"Fella gets killed, it's everybody's business," Big Al Henry said.

"Yessir," Randy said.

Henry turned to his foreman.

"Dan, I want you to find Adams."

"What for?"

"I want to talk to him."

"Why?"

"Just do it, damnit!" Henry said. "Don't question me."

"Sure, boss."

Robards put his barely touched beer down on the bar.

"Oh Christ, man," Henry said, "finish your beer first!"

"Yes, sir."

Robards picked up the mug again.

"I don't mean to yell at you," Henry said. "I'm just upset about the boy. He's a dimwit, but he wouldn't kill anybody."

"I know that, boss," Robards said. "Maybe a jury will see that, too."

"I don't want this goin' to a jury," Henry said. "Who knows how the boy will act in court?"

"It sounded to me like Judge Miller was gonna make sure this went to a jury."

"Well then," Henry said, "we're just gonna have to make sure it doesn't go to a jury."

"And you think the Gunsmith can help you with that?" Robards asked.

"I don't know," Henry said, "but the man is in town, and I want to talk to him. So do that for me, will you, Dan?"

"Sure, boss," Robards said. "Sure I will."

"We've got to get that boy out of jail," Al Henry said, more to himself than to anyone else. "Gotta get him out."

TEN

"What are we gonna do?" the deputy asked.

They had already talked with Terry Wilson, who had nothing to add to what they already knew. He was busy with three whores while Jason Henry was getting into trouble, and had apparently been fired because of it.

"What do you mean?"

"Well, Mr. Henry sure wants his boy outta jail," Ott said.

"What's that got to do with anything?" Brown asked.

"He's an important man in town."

"So that means I should open the cell and let his boy just walk out?" the sheriff demanded.

"Um . . . I would if I was sheriff."

"Okay, Sheriff," Brown said, whirling on the young deputy, "then what do you tell the judge?"

"Um . . ."

"And what would you have to say to Beth Collins?"

"Uh . . ."

"And what would you tell the citizens of this town about one of their own being murdered?"

"Um . . ."

"I guess it's a good thing you aren't the sheriff, isn't it?" Brown asked.

"Aw, I was just sayin'—"

"Well, don't just say," Brown said. "Think before you talk."

"Yessir."

"Go and see if the boy is eating his supper," Brown said. "Then go out and get us something."

"Where should I go?"

"I don't care," Brown said. "Go where you always ago."

"Yessir."

Ott went into the cell block, saw that Jason was busy eating his chicken, and then left the office to pick up supper for himself and the sheriff.

Clint found a small restaurant two blocks from the hotel. It was fairly busy, so he figured it must be pretty good. He went inside, got a table entirely too close to the front window, but it was all he could get. He sat facing the window, and the door, and placed his order for a steak. While he was waiting, he saw the deputy enter and talk to one of the waiters. He was probably ordering supper for the prisoner, or for himself and the sheriff.

Before he knew it, Clint was up and walking toward the young man. He decided he wasn't being nosy, he was just striking up a conversation.

"Is the food here any good?" he asked.

"Huh?" the deputy looked at him in surprise. "Oh, uh, Mr. Adams. Uh, sure. It's pretty good."

"I ordered a steak."

"It should be good," the deputy told him.

"Seems like a lot of activity going on in your office," Clint said.

"Huh?"

"I was sitting out in front of my hotel," Clint said. "Saw folks coming and going out of the sheriff's office."

"Oh, yeah," Ott said, "that was Big Al Henry—we got his son in a cell—and Judge Miller. Him and Big Al, they don't get along so good."

"I see. Who was the young woman?"

"Oh, that was Miss Beth," Ott said. "It was her pa who got killed."

"You think the fella you got in a cell did it?"

"That'd be Jason Henry," Ott said. "He's addled. Who knows what them folks do."

"Addled, huh?"

"Addled, slow," Ott said. "Folks call him different things."

"I see."

"He's a decent enough kid, 'bout seventeen or so."

"Think he's a killer?"

The deputy shrugged.

"I don't know about that," he said. "But I found him with the body, and there was a gun in the room. He coulda done it, I guess."

"It sounds like your sheriff's got a problem on his hands," Clint said.

"He sure does," Ott said. "Big Al's an important man around here, and he wants his boy outta jail."

"And I guess the judge is an important man, too, huh?" Clint asked.

"I guess so," Ott said, "and he wants the boy to go to trial."

"Sounds to me like the boy is going to trial."

"I guess . . ."

"Well," Clint said, "thanks for the advice."

"Advice?"

"About the food."

"Oh, yeah, uh, sure."

Clint went back to his table as the waiter was coming with his steak. Before long the deputy left with a covered tray.

"What did you get?" Sheriff Brown asked as the deputy entered the office.

"Uh, you didn't say what to get, so I brought fried chicken."

"That's fine."

Ott put the tray down on the desk and they each claimed a plate.

"Saw the Gunsmith in Gertie's," Ott said.

"What?"

"That's where I got the food, Gertie's Café," Ott said. "The Gunsmith was eatin' there."

"What did he want?"

"He just wanted to know if the food was any good there," Ott said.

"That's all?"

"Well . . . he did ask about what was happening in here," the deputy said. "Seems he was sittin' out in front of his hotel, across the street."

"And?"

Chewing on a chicken leg, Ott said, "He just saw folks comin' and goin', is all."

"And he was interested?"

"Naw," Ott said, "he was just makin' conversation."

"Just making conversation."

"Yeah."

Gesturing with a chicken leg of his own, Brown said, "You know, we better just hope he doesn't take an interest."

Ott stopped chewing.

"You think he might try to break the boy out?"

"Why would he?" Brown said. "You just said he wasn't interested."

"Yeah, but if he was," Ott said, "I don't wanna have to go against the Gunsmith for Jason Henry."

"Eat your chicken, Kenny," Brown said. "You're not going to have to go against the Gunsmith."

"Yeah, well, I hope not," Ott said.

"He's just passing through," Sheriff Brown said. "He doesn't have a dog in this fight."

Ott nodded, shrugged, bit into a chicken thigh.

Brown picked up a breast and bit into it. The Gunsmith said he was just passing through, but what if he wasn't? After all, Big Al Henry had enough money to hire anybody he wanted. The bartender said that Adams was drinking a beer when Collins was killed, so he couldn't have done it, but that didn't mean that Big Al couldn't hire him now to get his boy out of jail.

Brown dropped the chicken onto his plate, suddenly with no appetite.

ELEVEN

Clint's steak was okay, the coffee a bit weak. He decided to wash it all down with a beer or two, and crossed to the saloon.

It was fully busy now, with all the gaming tables going and the bar crowded with men drinking and laughing. As he approached the bar, though, somebody must have said something, because a space opened up for him before he even had to use an elbow. Then he saw that Randy was waiting for him, and knew what had happened.

"Beer?" Randy asked.

"Yes."

"Comin' up."

The men on either side of him gave him a wide berth. Randy had surely told them all who he was.

The bartender set a beer in front of Clint and said, "There ya go."

"Thanks."

He drank his beer, turned to survey the room. There

were three girls working the floor, and it looked like every other successful, busy saloon he'd ever been in.

"Lookin' to play?" Randy asked.

"Not right now."

"You just let me know when and I'll make sure a seat opens up for ya."

"I'll let you know."

He looked around, found that he was actually trying to see if Letty was there. The dirty-faced young woman was on his mind. He wondered what she'd look like after a bath.

"Lookin' for somebody?"

He turned his head, saw one of the saloon girls looking up at him. She was blond, a little chubby, with breasts that were overflowing from the top of her dress.

"Hello."

"You lookin' for somebody?" she asked again.

"No," he said, "I was just looking."

"Well," she said, "if you change your mind and decide to look for me, the name's Sally."

"Okay, Sally," he promised. "I'll remember."

She flounced away to serve beers to some of the saloon's patrons.

Dan Robards searched the town for Clint Adams, checking cafés and saloons, until he found him in Milty's. Nervously, he approached him at the bar.

"Mr. Adams?"

Clint turned at the sound of his name. He thought he recognized the man, but didn't know from where.

"Yes?"

"My name is Dan Robards."

"Do I know you?"

"No, sir," Robards said. "I'm the foreman at the Henry ranch, just outside of town."

"Oh yeah," Clint said, "now I remember. I saw you going into the sheriff's office today."

"That's right," Robards said, "with my boss, Mr. Al Henry."

"Big Al Henry, that's what I hear he's called."

"Right again."

"Can I buy you a beer?"

Robards was tempted, but he said, "No, thanks. Uh, fact is, been lookin' for you for a while." It was actually right in that same saloon earlier that his boss told him to look for Clint Adams.

"Oh? Why's that?"

"My boss—uh, Big Al—he'd like to talk to you."

"About what?"

"Actually, I don't know," Robards said. "He just told me to find you and ask you to talk with him."

"Wait a minute," Clint said, and signaled to Randy. When the bartender came over, he asked, "Randy, you know this fella?" He pointed to Robards.

"Sure, that's Dan Robards," Randy said. "He's Big Al Henry's foreman. Why?"

"He says Henry wants to see me."

"Well, fact is, I beard Big Al tell Dan here to find you for him."

"When was that?"

"Earlier in the day," the bartender said, "right here at this bar."

"Then he's on the up-and-up?"

"I'd say he is, yeah."

"Okay, thanks." Clint turned back to Robards. "Where is your boss now?"

"He took a room at the Ballard Hotel. It's, uh, the best one in town."

"I thought you said the ranch was right outside of town."

"It is," Robards said, "but he wants to be in town as long as his son's in jail."

"I see."

"Will you come and see him, sir?" Robards asked.

"Sure," Clint said. "Why not? I've got nothing better to do than drink some more beer."

"Big Al will have some good brandy and sippin' whiskey in his room."

"Well, that sounds good to me," Clint said. "Take me on over there."

"Thank you."

The two men left the saloon and Clint walked alongside the foreman as they made their way to the hotel. He didn't know what Big Al wanted with him, but he was kind of bored and decided to let the man talk.

He could do that and still manage to mind his own business, couldn't he?

TWELVE

The Ballard was twice the size of the hotel Clint was staying in. Big Al had apparently taken a suite that covered half of the third floor.

When they reached the door, Robards opened it without a key and led the way in. Clint found himself in an expensively furnished room, with heavy curtains and comfortable-looking furniture.

"I'll get the boss," Robards said.

"Sure."

The foreman left the room and came back moments later with the tall, white-haired man.

"Mr. Adams? I'm Al Henry."

"Big Al Henry, right?" Clint asked as they shook hands.

"That's not something I call myself," Henry said. "What about you and 'the Gunsmith'?"

"It's the same with me."

"Then you can just call me Al."

"Fine," Clint said, "I'm Clint."

"Can I get you a drink?"

"Your foreman said something about sippin' whiskey."

"From Kentucky," Henry said. "Have a seat and I'll get you a glass."

Clint noticed that the man poured a glass for Clint and for himself, but not for the foreman.

"What about Mr. Robards?" Clint asked as Henry handed him the glass.

"Oh, sure," Henry said. "Pour yourself a glass, Dan."

"Thanks," Robards said, more to Clint than to his boss.

Clint had chosen an armchair. So Al Henry sat on the overstuffed sofa. Robards, glass in hand, remained standing.

"I suppose you've been in town long enough to hear what's been going on?" Henry asked.

"About your son? Yes."

"I understand you haven't been real interested."

"No offense," Clint said, "but I've just been minding my own business."

"What if I asked you to make this your business?" Al Henry asked. "What if I offered to pay you to make it your business?"

"Then I'd have to ask you, how?" Clint asked. "What do you have in mind?"

"Actually," Big Al said, "I gotta tell you, I don't know yet. I just heard you were in town, and thought I should try to get you on my side."

"Instead of whose side?" Clint asked. "The law?"

"Judge Miller!" Henry said with distaste. "He thinks he's the law in this town, but he's not."

"Who is?" Clint asked. "You?"

"Of course not," Henry said. "The law is the law. Miller can't just interpret it the way he wants to."

"Well, maybe he can," Clint said. "After all, he is the judge."

"Well, he's not gonna railroad my son into prison," Henry said. "Jason could not have killed Ed Collins."

"Sounds like you need a detective," Clint said.

"We don't have a detective in town," Henry said, "and Miller's gonna push this through too quickly for me to bring somebody in. If I'm right about your background, you used to be a lawman."

"Many, many years ago," Clint said.

"Will you do it?" Henry asked. "Will you try to prove my son innocent?"

"I'm not a detective," Clint said, even though he had often worked with his friend Talbot Roper, who was possibly the best private detective in the country.

"I'll pay you ten thousand dollars to try," Al Henry said, "and another ten thousand if you succeed."

Twenty thousand dollars was powerful incentive, and if he accepted, it would be a job, not just him poking his nose into somebody else's business. And at least Big Al Henry wasn't offering him the money to try to break his son out of jail.

Clint sipped his whiskey.

"I tell you what," Henry said. "Take 'til morning to make up your mind. Come back here and have breakfast with me. They have an excellent dining room here. You can give me your answer then."

Clint set his empty glass down on a nearby table and stood up.

"I can do that, Al."

Henry stood up and the two men shook hands. As Clint headed for the door, Robards started to go with him. Clint held out his hand.

"I can find my way out of the hotel," he said. "Good night."

"Good night, sir," Henry said.

After Clint left, Robards turned to his boss.

"I thought you were going to offer him money to break Jason out," he said.

"I was," Henry said, "but I think this is better."

"How? He's not a detective."

"I'm still working on that," Henry said. "If he takes the job, he could be a distraction for both the sheriff and Miller."

"While we break him out?"

"Maybe," Henry said, "in the end I can get him to break Jason out if we have to. But I'll decide that later."

"We don't have much time," Robards reminded him.

"I know that," Big Al said, "but we can at least take tonight. You go back to the ranch tonight, make sure everything is all right there."

"And what do I tell Mrs. Henry?"

"Nothing," Henry said. "Just tell her I got busy and had to stay in town."

"Yes sir."

"Nothing more than that, Dan."

"Yessir."

"And I'll see you in the morning, after I have breakfast with Adams."

"I'll be here."

Henry slapped his foreman on the back and saw him to the door.

THIRTEEN

Clint went to his own room after seeing Big Al Henry. He removed his gun belt, hung it on the bedpost, then unbuttoned his shirt. It had been a long day of minding his own business, and in the end he was offered a job. He wondered what Rick Hartman would have to say about that.

He sat on the bed, removed his boots, then reclined on the bed with his hands behind his head. If he took the job, he was going to go and see the store where Ed Collins was killed, and he'd have to talk to Beth Collins about her father. Was the girl convinced that the killer was in jail? Or would she at least talk to him?

He was still trying to decide whether or not he should take the job—twenty thousand dollars was powerful incentive—when there was a knock on his door.

Clint didn't like knocks on the door. Too often it turned out to be a man with a gun. He took his gun from his holster and carried it to the door with him.

"Who is it?" he asked.

"It's me," a girl's voice said, "Letty."

"Letty?"

There was hesitation, then she said, "Dirty face."

"Oh," he said, "that Letty."

He held his gun behind his back and opened the door wide enough to look out. A girl he didn't remember ever seeing before was standing in the hall, alone.

"Letty?" he asked.

"That's me," she said, smiling.

The grin looked familiar, although he'd only seen it from behind a face full of grime.

He opened the door, looked both ways to make sure she was alone.

"You washed your face," he said.

"That ain't all," she told him. "Can I come in?"

He looked both ways again, then asked, "Does your uncle know you're here?"

"No," she said, "I don't tell him everythin' I do."

He looked at her again. He'd been right. She was pretty beneath the dirt.

"All right," he said. "Come on in before somebody sees you."

As she moved past him, the smell of soap drifted to his nose. He closed the door and turned to face her, his hand coming out from behind his back.

"You always answer the door with a gun in your hand?" she asked.

"Always," he said.

He walked to the bedpost and holstered it.

"What brings you here?" he asked.

"I wanted you to see me when I'm clean," she said.

"And how often is that?"

"Well, mostly when I ain't workin'."

"And what do you do when you're working that gets you so dirty?" he asked.

"Odd jobs," she said. "Whatever I can get. Somehow, though, I always seem to end up with dirty jobs."

"Well," he said, "you certainly look better with a clean face."

"That ain't all," she said. Suddenly her hands flew to her shirt and the buttons just seemed to come apart. She whipped the shirt off and tossed it away, and was naked to her waist.

"I also took a bath!"

He was stunned. Her breasts were small, but round like peaches, with pink nipples. Her skin was scrubbed clean, pale, and almost glowing.

"Letty . . ." he said, his mouth dry.

"Wait, wait," she said. Her hands went to her belt and her pants fell down around her ankles. She was naked now, except for the pants around her ankles, and her boots. Her whole body seemed to glow, and there was a bushy tangle of dark hair between her legs.

"See?" she said. "All clean."

He wondered if she knew what she was doing. Was she too innocent to realize that she had just become naked in a man's room? Or was she really here to seduce him into bed?

"Letty," he said, "do you know what you're doing?"

"Sure I do," she said, stepping out of her pants and kicking them away. "I'm tryin' to show ya that I'm a woman."

"Well," he said, "there's no doubt about that."

"Then," she said, "I think the next step is for us to get in that bed."

"Letty, your uncle—"

"My uncle don't have to know nothin'," she said. "He don't wanna admit that I'm a woman growed."

"Have you, uh, been with a man before?"

"Well, sure," she said, "I had a tumble or two in the hayloft with Billy Dunlop, but Billy left town. It's been a while."

"Left town?" Clint asked. "Or did your uncle chase him away?"

"It don't matter," she said. "Are you gonna come over here and help me take my boots off?"

Clint took a deep breath, acutely aware of the bulge in his trousers, and said, "I don't think I have much of a choice."

FOURTEEN

Terry Wilson was leaning on the bar at Milty's, his head hanging over a mug of beer, complaining to anyone who'd listen that he shouldn't have been fired.

"Goddamned kid," he muttered. "Why should I be blamed for what some addled kid does? Know what I mean?"

In this instance he was talking but nobody was listening to him. The only one who was paying any attention to him was Randy, the bartender.

"Hey, Terry, don't you think you had enough?"

Wilson raised his eyes to look at Randy.

"I picked up my pay, damn it," he said. "It's up to me how I wanna spend it, ain't it?"

"I guess so," Randy said.

"Then gimme another beer!"

Randy sighed, drew another beer for the man, and stuck it in front of him.

"You know what I should do?" Wilson asked.

This time Randy answered him, "What?"

"I oughtta put a bullet in Big Al Henry, see how he likes that! Ha!"

"That ain't the kinda thing you wanna be sayin' out loud, Terry," Randy said. "There's been enough trouble today with Ed Collins bein' killed."

"That wasn't my fault!"

"Nobody said it was."

"Oh yeah," Wilson said, "yeah, Big Al, he says it was my fault. And he fired me for it." He drank some beer. "I know who else I should put a bullet in."

"Who?" Randy asked.

"The kid," Wilson said, "Jason. That stupid kid."

"He ain't stupid," Randy said, "he's just a little slow. That's what they say."

"It don't matter what they say," Wilson said. "It's all that kid's fault, whether he pulled the trigger or not."

"You don't think he did?" the bartender asked.

"I dunno," Wilson said. "What do I care? All I know is, it ain't my fault."

"No," Randy said, "it probably ain't."

He left Wilson alone and moved down the bar. The saloon was starting to empty out and he looked around, trying to spot his niece, Letty. He hadn't seen much of her that night. He wondered what odd job she'd gotten for herself this time.

Clint leaned down as Letty lifted one foot so he could remove her boot. The movement brought her fragrant pubic patch close to his face. As he removed the second boot, he inhaled the smell of her. It was so sharp he knew she must already be wet.

She leaned her hands on his shoulders and he remained there on his knees. He reached around behind her, took her ass in his hands, and pulled her to him. He pressed his face into her bush, breathing her in deeply.

"Oh," she said, surprised. "Oh my."

He rubbed his face there, then pushed his tongue through the hair until he found her as wet as he had guessed.

"Oh!" she said, this time starting, as if she had been struck by lightning. He continued to lick her and she tightened her grip on his shoulders, digging in with her nails. "Oh God," she said, "Billy Dunlop never did that!"

He squeezed her buttocks in his hands, then abruptly stood up, lifting her with him. She wrapped her legs around him as he kissed her and, while kissing her, turned and carried her to the bed. Her tongue was avid in his mouth, her arms and legs tight around him. He had to virtually peel her off himself to put her down on the bed.

"Get undressed," she said breathily, "hurry, hurry . . ."

He hurried, pulling his clothes off and tossing them aside. When he removed his underwear, his erection sprang out at her and her eyes widened.

"Billy Dunlop sure didn't have that!" she said.

"He didn't have one?" he asked.

"Well, he did," she said, "but his tallywacker was kind of . . . well, small."

She reached out, took it in one hand, then also wrapped the other hand around it.

"Oh my!" she said as it filled her hands.

"Let me show you what to do with that," he said, reaching for her . . .

FIFTEEN

Judge Frank Miller sat at his desk in his four-column, Southern-style, two-family home on the edge of town. The house was quiet, as it had been for fifteen years since the death of his dear wife, May. In the beginning, he'd missed her and had been lonely. Now, however, he enjoyed the peace and quiet of the large, silent house and would never have wanted to live with anyone else.

The only time he heard sounds in the house was during the day, when his cook was there. But she left the house right after dinner. She was not even allowed to clean up her kitchen until the next morning, when she arrived for a new day of work.

Miller had several cases on his docket, but the one he was most concerned with was the case of Jason Henry. Whether the boy had actually shot and killed Ed Collins or not, this was Miller's chance to finally get the upper hand on Big Al Henry. The two had been fencing for years, ever since their friendship had come to an end.

The boy was an idiot. He would be no loss if Miller succeeded in sending him to prison, or to the gallows. In the morning Miller would be meeting with David House, who was the attorney who would be prosecuting the boy. He had no idea who Big Al would be getting to defend his boy, but Miller wasn't going to give him time to bring in somebody from out of town. He was going to have to choose from the few attorneys who lived in town, all of whom were intimidated by Judge Miller.

Miller closed the file on his desk and stood up. He was wearing a silk dressing gown in lavender, belted around his corpulent middle. He poured himself a glass of brandy, carried it from the office with him, to his bedroom.

Tomorrow would be the beginning of the end for Big Al Henry.

There was no way he was going to get his addled boy off the hook for this murder.

"Wow," Letty said breathlessly, "I ain't never done that to Billy Dunlop's tallywacker. Didn't even know I could do that. You sure are a tasty man, Clint Adams."

They were lying side by side on the bed. Clint had his hand on her crotch, playing gently with her moist public hair. She had his semi-erect penis in her hand and was just stroking it.

"Letty, sweetie, can you do me a great big favor?" he asked without looking at her.

"Sure, Clint," she said. "Anything."

"Could you keep Billy Dunlop out of this bed for the rest of the night?"

"Sure," she said. "I can do that."

"Good."

After a few seconds she said, "The rest of the night? Am I gonna be here the rest of the night?"

"Well," he said, rolling toward her, "I guess that's up to you."

Sheriff Gordon Brown stood up from his desk and walked into the cell block. He looked into Jason Henry's cell and saw that the boy was lying there, awake.

"You need anything, Jason?" he asked.

"I need to go home, Sheriff."

"Sorry, boy," Brown said. "I can't do that, but do you want anything else?"

The boy sniffed the air.

"Is that coffee I smell?"

"Sure is," Brown said. "I just made a cup. You want some?"

"That would be great, Sheriff."

"Okay. I got no cream, but do you want sugar?"

"Naw, just nice and black and strong."

"Comin' up."

Brown went to the potbellied stove and poured two tin cups full with coffee. He carried them back to the cell block, set Jason's down, balanced on the cell door.

"There you go."

Jason got up from his cot and took the cup from the door. Brown had stepped back so the boy wouldn't be tempted to toss it in his face. That had happened before.

Jason sat on the cot and sipped the coffee.

"So tell me, Jason," Brown said, leaning against the wall with his coffee.

"Yessir?"

"Did you kill Ed Collins?"

"No sir, I didn't," Jason said.

"Then who did?"

"I don't know, sir," Jason said. "I swear."

"Then tell me again what happened."

"I started to go in the back room," Jason said. "Somebody grabbed me around the throat and then . . . I woke up next to Mr. Collins. I really thought he was sleeping."

"Okay," Brown said, "you told me everything you told me before. Now tell me something else."

"Something else?"

"Something you haven't told me yet."

"Like what?"

"I don't know, Jason," Brown said. "I'm trying to help you here. Something you saw, or felt, or smelled—"

"Smelled!" Jason said, his eyes going wide.

"What?" Brown asked. "What did you smell?"

"Somebody," Jason said, "somebody smelled really . . . good."

"Good?"

"Sweet," Jason said. "I smelled something sweet."

"You were in the back room of the mercantile," Brown said. "I'm sure there was something sweet back there."

"No," Jason said, "it wasn't something sweet I smelled. It was some . . . one!"

SIXTEEN

Daniel Thayer slapped Stephanie Kitten on her bare rump, withdrew from her sopping pussy, and shot his seed over her back.

And he was done.

Stephanie had not even gotten started. She knew she was going to have to leave Thayer's house and go find herself a man—any man—who could last longer than he could.

That wouldn't be very hard.

She rolled over to lie on her back, which would effectively wipe him off on his own sheets.

He got off the bed, grabbed his silk dressing robe, and pulled it on.

"You did a fine job today," he told her.

She finished drying her back on his sheets and moved over to get away from the wetness.

"That's what you pay me for."

"How did you hit on framing the boy?"

"He walked in," she said. "I didn't have much of a choice."

"Well, Collins is gone," Thayer said. "That's what I wanted. I'll go and talk to the grieving daughter and offer to help her get rid of her daddy's store."

"What makes you think she won't want to run it?"

"She's never worked in there a day in the last three years," he said. "As soon as she got old enough to go her own way, she started her own store. She's not going to want to go anywhere near it."

"What about Big Al?"

"I thought about that," he said, "but Big Al's going to be busy trying to get his boy out of jail. You actually did me a favor by getting him off my back."

"I'll bet I made Judge Miller's day, too," Stephanie said.

Thayer poured himself a glass of brandy and laughed.

"I'll bet you did." He walked to the chest of drawers, took an envelope from the top drawer. "When you get dressed, you can have your money."

She got off the bed and started dressing. He didn't even watch her. She was used to men watching her all the time—but not Daniel Thayer.

When she was dressed, she walked to him and accepted the envelope from him. It was appropriately thick.

"Stick around town," Thayer said. "I may need you for something else."

She put the envelope of cash in her back pocket, and strapped on her gun.

"I'll be around," she said.

She went out the door, eager for a bath to get the rest of Thayer's scum off her back.

* * *

Stephanie's two partners were not waiting for her this time when she came out of the house. That was okay with her. She was so ready for a man, she might have taken one of them to bed, and that would have been the end of their partnership. She never slept with men she was partnered with.

Also, since they weren't waiting for her, she had a chance to skim some of the money off the top before she gave them their shares. Not that they deserved any of it. She had done all the work. She always did.

She headed home so she could take a bath with that new sweet-smelling soap she had bought and then she was going to go out and find herself a man who could last more than a minute with her.

Stephanie's partners, Tony Black and Andy Choate, were sitting and drinking in a small saloon called Scott's. The rest of the customers had left more than half an hour ago, and the place was officially closed. Fact was, Scott was a friend of theirs who let them drink as long as they wanted to.

Scott—who was the same age as Tony and Stephanie, mid-thirties—came over and sat down with them.

"Come on, Tony," he said, "tell me how that Stephanie is in bed. Come on."

"I told you, Scott," Tony said, "a gentleman never tells."

"Aw, you ain't no gentleman, Tony," Andy said, grinning. "Tell 'im."

"Never mind," Tony said. "Just finish your beer. And you, Scott, finish cleanin' your bar."

"You boys finish up, then," Scott said. "I gotta lock up and go home. The wife is waitin'."

"So tell me, Scott," Tony said, "how's that wife of yours in bed, huh?"

"She's a cold fish, Tony," Scott said, standing up. "That's why I keep askin' you about Stephanie. That is one hot woman. Does she wear that gun belt in bed?"

"Never mind, Scott."

"Ah," the saloon owner said, and went back to cleaning his bar.

"You're drivin' that guy crazy," Andy said.

"Just don't you tell him I ain't got Steph into bed yet, that's all."

"And you never will."

"I'm workin' on her," Tony said. "Just wait and see. The day will come."

"That day ain't never gonna come," Andy said.

"You got money to put on that?"

"I got a hundred dollars says you never get her into bed," Andy said. "Never."

"You got a bet," Tony said.

"You guys," Scott yelled from the bar. "Time to go home and get some sleep."

"Yeah," Tony said, "time to go and get some sleep. We got a new day tomorrow."

"And get our share of the money from Steph," Andy said.

"Yeah," Tony said, "that, too."

SEVENTEEN

Letty was obviously not experienced when it came to sex, so Clint went slow with her, showed her a few things—all of which she took to immediately.

Eventually, Letty wanted to go faster, and he obliged. She especially liked sitting on top of his cock, riding him until he exploded deep inside her.

She literally fell off him at one point when they were both done, and they lay side by side in bed, catching their breath.

"Oh my God," she said. "I'm gonna have to have sex every day after this."

"Not every day," Clint said. "You do that and the word will get around. You don't want your uncle to know."

"God, no!" she said. "If Uncle Randy found out, he'd kill any man I was with."

"Including me," Clint said.

"Oh, I'm not gonna tell him about you," she assured him. "I'm not done with you yet, so I don't want you dead."

"I don't want me dead either."

"So how long are you gonna be in town?" she asked.

"I don't know," Clint said. "I was only passing through, but it might change."

"Why?" she asked.

"I've been offered a job," he said.

"Are you gonna take it?"

"I don't really know," he said, "but I have to decide by morning."

"Well," she said, snuggling up to him, "if it keeps you here longer, I hope you take the job."

"I need some time to think about it," he said, "so why don't you go to sleep and I'll do that."

"I am pretty tired," she said, closing her eyes. "Can I stay all night?"

"Sure you can," he said, "as long as Uncle Randy doesn't find out."

Sleepily, she said, "He won't ever find out . . . not from me anyway."

In moments, she was asleep.

Clint's intention was to give Big Al Henry's job offer some pretty serious thought, but a few moments after Letty fell asleep, so did he.

Clint awoke in the morning to find Letty down between his legs, nuzzling his cock to life. When it was fully hard, she took it into her mouth, sucked it avidly for a while before mounting him and riding him again.

"Oh, Lord!" she said, hopping off him. "I have to get home and take a bath! I bet I stink."

"Well," he said as she started to dress, "at least you're not dirty."

"If you're gonna stay around town for a while, I'll make sure I'm always clean," she said, "no matter what job I take."

"That's a deal," he said.

She paused as she was pulling on her trousers and looked over at him.

"So you're gonna take that job?"

"I think so," he said. "I have to talk with the man again this morning."

Letty finished dressing, went to the bed, and kissed him.

"I'll see you at Milty's."

"Hey, about that," Clint said. "Who's Milty?"

"He used to own the saloon. He died last year, and left the place to my uncle, who was his bartender."

"Why doesn't he change the name?"

"It's the best-known saloon in town," she said. "I guess he just didn't think it was smart to do."

"Probably right."

"I gotta go," she said. "See you later."

She ran out the door.

Clint got off the bed immediately, washed with the pitcher and basin in the room, got dressed, and left his room to go and meet Al Henry for breakfast.

Big Al Henry came down to the lobby of his hotel and stopped at the front desk.

"Any messages?" he asked the clerk.

"No, sir, Mr. Henry."

"All right," he said. "If anyone's looking for me, I'll be having breakfast."

"Yessir."

He walked to the dining room, which was about half

full that early. A waiter showed him to his regular table.
He always sat in the same place when he was in town.

Across the room from him he saw Daniel Thayer having breakfast alone. There was some debate in town over
who was a wealthier man, he or Thayer. Big Al had no
opinion on the subject. Thayer looked over at him and
nodded. He returned the nod.

"The usual, Mr. Henry?" a waiter asked.

"I'm waiting for a guest, Gary," he said. "Just bring me
a pot of coffee."

"Yessir."

Big Al hoped that this day was going to start the way
he wanted it to, with the Gunsmith in his employ. Once
word of that employment reached Judge Miller, maybe he
would gain some semblance of balance again. He hated to
think that Miller had any sort of advantage over him, but
as long as his son was in jail, that would probably be the
case.

The waiter came with the coffee, poured him a cup, and
Big Al settled back to wait for the Gunsmith.

EIGHTEEN

When Clint walked into the hotel dining room, Al Henry spotted him and waved him over.

"Good morning," Henry said.

"Morning," Clint said as they shook hands.

"Have some coffee. I waited for you before ordering."

"Thanks."

Clint poured the coffee, found it strong enough for him. The waiter came over and Clint said, "Steak and eggs."

"Yes, sir. Mr. Henry?"

"Eggs Benedict, Gary."

"Yessir."

"I discovered eggs Benedict when I first went to New York," Henry explained.

"I've had them before," Clint said. "Didn't care for them much."

"Where did you have them?" the rancher asked.

"Also in New York," Clint said.

"Do you go to New York often?"

"I've been there a few times," Clint said.

Al Henry sipped his coffee, then put his cup down and said, "Small talk is painful, isn't it?"

"It can be," Clint said.

"Have you made up your mind about the job?" Big Al asked.

"I'll take it—"

"Good!"

"With a couple of conditions."

"What are they?"

"I do things my way."

"Agreed."

"And the sheriff has to agree."

"The sheriff? Why?"

"I don't want to be at odds with the law."

"But you'll be at odds with Judge Miller."

"As far as I'm concerned," Clint said, "the judge doesn't come into this until and unless it goes to court. Sheriff Brown is the law."

"Well," Big Al said, "I don't see why he'd object."

"I'll talk to him today," Clint said. "If he warns me off, I'll have to turn the job down."

"If that's the way you want it," Henry said.

"That's the way it has to be."

"All right," Henry said. "When will you talk to Sheriff Brown?"

"Right after breakfast."

"And then you'll let me know?"

"Right away."

"All right," Henry said. "If you need my help with the investigation—just my help, mind you—let me know."

"I will."

"After you've talked with the sheriff, if you accept the job, we'll take a walk over to my bank."

"Fine."

The waiter came with their plates and set them down.

"How about some champagne with breakfast?" Big Al asked.

"Sure," Clint said, "why not?"

After breakfast, Clint left Big Al still drinking champagne at the table while he walked over to the sheriff's office. As he entered, he saw Sheriff Brown sitting behind his desk. Deputy Ott was nowhere in sight.

"Morning, Sheriff."

"Good morning, Mr. Adams. What can I do for you?"

"I just had breakfast with Big Al Henry."

"I hope he paid."

"He did."

"And?"

"He's hired me to prove his son's innocence."

"And if he isn't innocent?"

"I'll tell Big Al that, too."

"Are you a detective?"

"Not exactly," Clint said, "but I've worked with some good detectives. What I need to know is, do you object?"

"Hell, no, I don't object," Brown said. "Go ahead and prove he's innocent. But at the same time, try to prove who's guilty, will you? That's the only way I'll be able to keep Judge Miller off my back."

"Maybe we can work together on this."

"That's not very likely," Brown said. "Judge Miller wouldn't like it."

"Is he your boss?"

"He's the judge."

"But you work for the town, right?" Clint asked. "As in, the town council? The mayor?"

"They're all afraid of Judge Miller," Brown said. "Everybody is."

"Are you?"

Sheriff Brown hesitated, then said, "Let's just say I like my job."

"I get it."

"So I can't help you," Brown said, "but I won't stand in your way."

"Good," Clint said. "I'd like to go into the cell block and talk to the boy."

"Jason Henry."

"Right."

"Sure," Brown said, "just leave your gun on my desk and go ahead."

Clint took his gun from his holster reluctantly, set it down on the desk, and said, "Thanks."

He went into the cell block to start his new job.

NINETEEN

Clint walked into the cell block, saw Jason Henry sitting on his cot, staring at the floor.

"Jason?"

The boy looked up quickly.

"I'm Clint Adams," Clint said. "Would you mind if we talked?"

"I don't mind," Jason said. "It's pretty lonely in here. Whataya wanna talk about?"

"Your father has asked me to try and prove that you didn't kill Mr. Collins."

"I didn't kill him," Jason said.

"And I'm going to believe you," Clint said. "Your dad says you couldn't have done it. But I need you to give me something I can use to prove it."

"Like what?"

"Something you saw, or heard."

"Or smelled?"

"You smelled something?"

"Yes."

Clint waited, and when it was clear the boy wasn't going to volunteer the information he asked, "What?"

"Well, something sweet . . . or someone."

"Like . . . a person?"

"Yeah," Jason said, "like . . . maybe soap?"

And who would smell like sweet soap? Certainly not a man.

"You think there was a woman there?"

"Maybe," Jason said.

"Okay," Clint said, "I know you've gone through this before, but very slowly tell me everything that happened."

"Well, my dad sent me to town to buy supplies . . ."

Clint listened intently while the boy told him the whole story. When he finished, there was a silent moment between them.

"Okay," Clint said, "the arm that went around your neck . . . that couldn't have been a woman's arm, could it?"

"I don't think so," the boy said. "It was so strong!"

"So," Clint said, "maybe there were two people there, a man and a woman."

"Maybe . . ."

"You didn't hear any voices?"

"No," Jason said. "I was the only one talking, yelling for Mr. Collins."

It would have helped if the boy had remembered at least one voice.

"And the store was empty?"

"Yeah," Jason said, "totally empty. I ain't never seen it like that before."

"That couldn't be a coincidence," Clint said, speaking

to himself, but aloud so that Jason could hear it. "Maybe when the real killers walked in, somebody saw them. I just have to ask some of the store's regular customers."

"How will you know who they are?"

"Mr. Collins must have kept record of who his regulars were," Clint said, "especially if he extended them credit. And I understand he has a daughter?"

"Miss Beth," Jason said, "but she doesn't work in the store."

"If it's locked, though, she's the one who would have to let me in," Clint said. "Do you know where she lives?"

"Right upstairs from the store."

"Good," Clint said, "maybe I'll find her there. Did you tell anyone else about what you smelled?"

"Sure," Jason said, "I told Sheriff Brown."

"You did?" Clint asked. "When was that?"

"Just last night."

The sheriff wouldn't have had any time to act on that information yet.

"Okay," Clint said, "I guess I'll get started, then."

"How soon do you think you can get me out?" Jason asked.

"I don't know, Jason," Clint said, "but you can depend on the fact that I'm working on it—thanks to your dad."

"I can't wait to go back home," he said.

"I'm sure your mother misses you," Clint said.

"My mother's dead," Jason said. "She died when I was little. Nancy is my stepmother."

"Well," Clint said, "then I'm sure she's worried. I'll be back soon."

"Okay, Mr. Adams. Thanks."

Clint went back out and picked up his gun from the

sheriff's desk. He decided not to mention what the boy had told him about the sweet-smelling soap. Maybe the sheriff had his own ideas about it, but he didn't really want to hear them. He had his own investigation to conduct.

"Can you tell me if the mercantile is locked?"

"I guess it is."

"Then I'll have to go to Beth Collins so she can let me in."

"I suppose . . ."

"No objection?"

Brown shook his head and said, "None."

"Okay, then," Clint said. "I'll be in touch."

"Good," the lawman said. "Let me know how things go. And watch out for the judge."

"I will," Clint said. "Thanks for the warning."

"You might also," Brown said as Clint headed for the door, "be careful around Big Al Henry."

"Big Al?"

"Yeah," Brown said. "I know you're working for him, but he and the judge will do anything to get at each other. Big Al will sacrifice anyone, even you."

"And his son?"

"Sadly," Brown said, "I think so."

"I'll keep that in mind, Sheriff," Clint said. "Thanks."

TWENTY

Clint tried the front door of the mercantile first, just in case it was unlocked. It wasn't. He walked around to the side and found a stairway that led to the second floor. He went up and knocked on the door. There was no answer. When he came down, he found himself facing a middle-aged woman with a stern expression on her face.

"Who are you?" she demanded.

"My name is Clint Adams," he said. "I was looking for Beth Collins."

"She just lost her father, you know," the woman said.

"I do know that," Clint said. "I wanted to talk to her about it."

"Well, I have the store on this side," she said. "I'm just keepin' an eye on the place."

"That's very nice of you."

"Beth has her own shop a few streets down," the woman said. "She didn't want to work in her father's store, so she opened her own."

"So you think she'll be there?"

"I do," she said. "That girl won't stop working, even though her father's dead."

"Well, I thank you for the information, ma'am," Clint said. "I'll just go down there and talk to her."

"You be kind to her," the woman said. "That girl's been through enough."

"I will be kind, ma'am," he said. "I promise."

As he started to walk away, she called out, "And you should know she's available."

"Uh, thank you."

"And pretty," the woman called.

He waved and kept going.

Beth Collins's store turned out to be a haberdashery shop. The window had some articles of clothing in it, but he knew that a haberdasher was someone who dealt in buttons and bows and things of that nature.

He entered and a small bell tinkled to announce his arrival. There were four women in the store, and they all turned to look at him.

"Hello," he said. "I'm looking for Beth Collins."

The women—of varying ages from sixteen to sixty—looked at each other, apparently trying to decide who the spokesperson should be, and doing so without uttering a word.

"She's in the storeroom," an older woman finally said. "She'll be back shortly."

"Thank you," he said. "I'll wait."

The women exchanged glances again, and then the older woman approached him. She was a handsome, gray-haired woman who had obviously been a beauty in her youth.

"You do know that her father was just murdered yesterday?" she asked.

"I do," he said. "In fact, that's what I'm here to talk to her about."

"Why?" the woman asked.

"I'd like to find out who killed him."

"We know who killed him," a younger woman asked. She came forward, a rather stern-looking woman of forty or so. "That addled boy, Jason Henry."

"That's right," a woman in her thirties said. "He's in jail right now."

"I know," Clint said, "but his father doesn't think he did it."

"I don't think so either," the sixteen-year-old said.

The other women all looked at her.

"I'm sorry," she said, "he's a sweet boy."

"A sweet killer," the older woman said. "You have to watch out for those sweet ones."

"Yeah," the forty-year-old said.

"What's going on?" Beth Collins asked as she came back into the room. "I thought I heard a man—oh."

"Miss Collins," Clint said. "My name is Clint Adams. I'm here to talk to you about your father's death—that is, if you'll talk to me."

"About what?"

"About who killed your father."

"I know who killed my father."

"That's what we told him," the older woman said.

"Yeah," the forty-year-old said.

"Mama," the sixteen-year-old said to her.

"I think everyone should leave," Beth announced. "I obviously need to talk to this man."

"Are you sure you want to be alone with him?" the forty-year-old asked.

"Yes, I am," Beth said. "Thank you all for your concern."

As she actively ushered the four women from her store, Clint heard the older woman say, in a low voice, "I know I wouldn't mind being alone with him."

"Oh, Regina!" Beth said.

Beth got the women out the door and locked it behind her. She turned and came back into the store. Clint was impressed with her. She couldn't have been more than twenty-one or -two, but she had great maturity about her.

"Now what can you possibly have to ask me about my father's death, Mr. Adams?"

"Have you heard Jason's story, Miss Collins?"

"I have not," she said. "I heard that he was found standing over my father's dead body with a gun in his hand."

"That's not quite right," Clint said. "He was unconscious when your father was killed, and there was a gun in the room. That's hardly incriminating."

"That is not what I heard."

"Well," Clint said, "maybe you should hear his side of it, then."

She hesitated, then said, "All right, perhaps I should."

TWENTY-ONE

Clint told Beth the story Jason had told her, and she listened intently.

"So you want to go to my father's store and take a look?" she asked when he was done. That was not exactly the reaction he had been hoping for.

"Yes, I do," he said. "I tried the door, but it's locked, and the sheriff has no objection."

"All right," she said. "Let me get the keys and I'll take you over there."

She went into the back room, came back with a set of keys. They left her store and started down the street.

"I ran into a very protective woman after I knocked on your door above the mercantile."

She grinned—a grin that came and went too quickly— and said, "That's Mrs. Mason. She had her eye on my dad for her next husband."

"Next? How many has she had?"

"Five," she said. "She's managed to outlive them all. Now she outlived my father before they could even get married."

"Was he thinking of marrying her?"

"I don't think so," she said, "but I would never tell her that. It would shake her confidence."

"Well," Clint said, "we wouldn't want to do that, would we?"

When they reached the store, Beth unlocked the door and entered, Clint close behind her. As they entered, he noted that she smelled fresh, but not sweet, so it hadn't been her in that back room—unless she'd smelled different the day before.

That made him think of something.

Before they went in any further, he grabbed her arm, startling her.

"I'm sorry," he said, "but I wanted to stop you before you were inside any further. Have you been in the store since yesterday?"

"No," she said, "I couldn't—I just locked it up."

"You smell good," he said.

"I don't think this is the time—"

"No, what I mean is, I want to see if I can smell what the boy smelled, so would you do me a favor and wait outside for a few moments?"

"Oh, I see. Yes, of course."

"I'll come and get you after I've taken a walk through," he promised.

She backed out of the store, and he closed the door.

He went directly to the back room, since that was where

the action had taken place. Brushing aside the curtain, he stepped through the doorway and stopped. He inhaled, but as he had suspected—or been afraid of—the smell of whatever Jason Henry had detected had dissipated.

He went back through the store and opened the front door.

"It's okay," he said. "The smell is gone."

"What did it smell like?" she asked, coming back inside.

"Jason said it was sweet, like soap."

Her eyes widened.

"A woman?" she asked. "A woman killed my father? Is that what you're saying?"

"Either that, or there was a man and a woman," Clint said. "Jason was pretty insistent that the arm that choked him was strong, like a man's arm."

As they reached the curtained doorway, she stopped.

"I don't want to go back there."

"I understand," he said. "I'm just going to go in and walk around a bit, see what I can see."

"All right."

"Meanwhile," he said, "I'd like to talk to some of your father's regular customers. Is there a list somewhere?"

"Yes," she said, "Dad had a book with the names and addresses of all the people he extended credit to. I guess those are the people you'll want."

"Good," he said. "Would you see if you can find that?"

"I know where it is," she said.

He nodded, went back through the curtain again.

He looked down at the floor, where there was a dry bloodstain. Just as well Beth had not accompanied him back there.

Walking around the room, he didn't really know what he was looking for. So he stood across from the doorway and tried to envision what had happened.

There were at least two people back there with Ed Collins, a man and a woman. They heard Jason Henry enter, and the boy called out for Collins. The man must have moved to stand next to the doorway, and when the boy stuck his head in, the man wrapped his arm around his neck and choked him out.

While the boy was on the floor unconscious, the man and woman killed Ed Collins for some reason. They then left the boy there next to the dead body to be discovered and blamed.

But the boy could have awakened and left the store. Apparently when he did wake up, he remained there, staring at Collins, maybe trying to revive him, since he thought he was asleep. The deputy found him there, crouched over the body—but not with a gun in his hand. According to the sheriff, he only found the gun beneath Collins's body when some men lifted it.

That brought up a few questions Clint had to think about.

He went back into the store, found the girl behind the counter.

"I found my father's account book," she said.

"Good. Let's take that with us."

"Are you finished here?" she asked.

"Yes," he said, "I've got some things to think about."

"Where are you going to do that?"

"I don't know," he said, "maybe in a saloon over a beer, or a café over some coffee—"

"I've got a better idea," she said. "Come upstairs and I'll make coffee. We can go right up those stairs." She pointed to a stairway he hadn't seen, against the wall. It blended in.

It was an offer he couldn't refuse.

TWENTY-TWO

While Clint followed Beth Collins up the stairs to the rooms she'd shared with her father, Daniel Thayer entered Judge Frank Miller's office.

"Daniel," Miller said. "Have a seat. Can I get you a drink?"

"Some of that fine brandy you have?" Thayer asked.

"Done."

Miller poured two glasses of brandy without having to rise from his chair, and slid one across the desk to Thayer.

"What's on your mind, Daniel?" Judge Miller asked.

"I heard about Ed Collins being killed," Thayer said. "Is it true that Big Al's addled son did it?"

"That's how it looks."

"As he going to trial?"

"Just as soon as I can schedule it."

"Big Al must be upset."

"Beside himself."

The two men grinned and clinked glasses across the desk.

"And what about Collins's store?" Thayer asked. "What's going to happen to that?"

"If you still want to buy it," Miller said, "I think you'll have to take that up with his daughter."

"Is she old enough to make that deal?"

"She is," Miller said. "I believe she's twenty."

"I'll take it up with her, then," Thayer said.

"After an appropriate time, of course," the judge said.

"Of course."

The two men toasted each other again.

Stephanie never found a man the night before.

She had gone home, had her bath with her new sweet-smelling soap, but by the time she got back out on the street, the saloons were empty. At least, there were no men she'd take home to her bed, not even for a quick poke.

She went home to bed and woke up the next morning in a bad mood.

She dressed, strapped on her gun, and went outside. Down the street was a small café that didn't have very good food, but it was owned by Andy Choate's mother, so they usually met there.

When she walked in, Choate and Tony Black were sitting there, drinking coffee.

"You missed breakfast," Tony said.

"Never mind," Choate's mother, Mary, said, coming up behind her. "She can have whatever she wants."

"Thank you, Mary," Stephanie said. "I'll have a Spanish omelet, please."

"Comin' up. Andrew, pour Stephanie some coffee.

Where are your manners?" She patted Stephanie on the shoulder and said, "You smell very sweet, dear."

"Thank you, Mary. It's my new soap."

Stephanie sat down, and after Choate poured her a cup of coffee, she sipped it.

"We get our money?" Tony asked.

Stephanie looked around. She had, indeed, missed breakfast, and the place was empty except for them, so she took out their money and handed it to each of them.

"Any more jobs?" Choate asked.

"Maybe," Stephanie said. "We'll just stick around town to wait and see."

"Well, I heard somethin'," Black said.

"What's that?" Stephanie asked.

"Clint Adams is in town."

"The Gunsmith?" Choate asked. "What's he want here?"

"I don't know," Black said, "but he was seen eating breakfast with Big Al Henry."

"Damnit!" Stephanie said. "Big Al's gonna hire him."

"To do what?" Choate asked.

"I don't know," Stephanie said, "but I don't like it."

"So what do we do?" Choate asked.

"Nothin'," Stephanie said. "Unless we hear from Thayer."

"Why don't we check Adams out ourselves?" Tony Black asked.

"You and Andy stay away from him, Tony," Stephanie said. "If anybody's gonna check on him, it'll be me."

"You ain't gonna try him, are you, Steph?" Choate asked.

"I don't know," Stephanie said.

"You're not ready for the Gunsmith, Steph," Tony said.

"Thanks for the vote of confidence, Tony."

"I would like to know," Black said, "what the hell he's doin' in Copper Canyon."

"Well," Stephanie said as Mary Choate came out with her omelet, "maybe we'll find out."

Sheriff Brown was sitting back in his chair when Deputy Ott came in.

"It's about time," Brown said, taking his feet off his desk and standing. "I've got to go out. Keep an eye on the kid."

"What are you gonna do?"

"Never mind," Brown said. "I'll be back soon."

"Can I let anybody see him?" Ott asked.

"Yes," Brown said, "let his father see him, and Clint Adams."

"Adams?"

"He's working for Big Al."

Ott looked surprised.

"Big Al hired a gun?"

"Not exactly," Brown said. "Look, Kenny, just sit your butt behind the desk until I get back, and don't worry so much about everything."

"Sure, Sheriff," Ott said.

TWENTY-THREE

Upstairs Beth excused herself and went into the kitchen, leaving Clint in a small sitting room. Off to one side he saw two doorways he assumed led to small bedrooms. He wondered how two people could live up there.

"I don't have coffee," she called from the kitchen. "Will you take tea?"

"Sure."

"And I have some cookies."

"That sounds great."

She came walking in a short time later, set down a tray of tea and cookies on the table in front of the sofa.

"Come sit here," she said.

He obeyed, sitting next to her as she poured the tea into cups. The cookies were oatmeal, and they were very good.

"You make these?" he asked.

"Yes, I did . . . they were my father's favorite."

He stopped chewing and stared at her.

"No, no," she said, "it's fine. Keep eating them. I'd like them to be enjoyed."

"Oh, okay," he said, and continued to chew.

"So," she said, "what did you find out downstairs?"

"Not much, I'm afraid," he said. "I didn't smell anything, or find anything, but if Jason is telling the truth, it looks like there was more than one killer."

"How many?"

"At least two, a man and a woman," Clint said.

"Maybe more?"

"Maybe."

She picked up her cup and sipped her tea.

"If this is too difficult for you—"

"No, no," she said, "not at all. What's difficult for me is to think that I immediately blamed that poor boy for my father's death, when I should have known better."

"Should have?"

"I know that Jason is a sweet boy," she said, "and that he has some . . mental problems. He'd have no reason to kill my father. I just . . . I was upset, and when I was told he was the killer, I . . .it was just easier for me to believe it."

"And who told you that?"

"Judge Miller."

"Why would the judge tell you that and not the sheriff?"

"The judge came to my shop to tell me what happened," she said. "He said he wanted to be . . . helpful." She frowned. "That should have been another tip-off."

"Oh? Why?"

"My father and Judge Miller were on the town council together," she said, "and they never got along."

"Is that a fact?" Clint said. He sipped some tea. "Who else is on the town council?"

"Well, there's Daniel Thayer, Big Al Henry, a few other storekeepers. But most of the talking is usually done by Big Al, Thayer, the judge, and . . ."

"And your father?"

"Yes."

"And tell me," Clint said, "who did your father usually side with? When it came to voting, and making decisions?"

"Big Al and my dad were usually on one side, while the judge and Thayer were on the other."

"That's very interesting."

"Are you saying my father was killed because of something that went on in town council meetings?"

"I don't know," Clint said. "Could be."

"That poor boy," she said again. "Can you get him out of jail?"

"Probably not," Clint said. "Judge Miller is determined to try him. I can't just get him out. I have to prove he didn't do it, and then . . ."

"And then prove who did?"

"Yes."

"Well," she said, setting her cup down, "how can I help?"

"You've already helped," he said.

"How?"

"By letting me into the store."

"But you didn't find anything."

"I got a look at the scene of the crime," Clint said. "I can see how Jason would have been choked if he put his head through the doorway. Especially if they were waiting for him."

"Why would they wait for him?"

"To frame him."

"Who would want to frame him for my father's murder?" she asked.

"That's the question," he said.

"How are you going to get the answer?"

"By asking more questions."

"Of whom?"

"Well," he said "to start with, members of the town council."

"Including Judge Miller?"

"Including Judge Miller."

He swallowed the last bit of his second cookie and washed it down with the last of his tea.

"You're going to go up against Judge Miller? In this town?" she asked.

"I'm going to do what I have to do to prove that boy innocent," he said.

"If you go against the judge," she said, "you'll also be going against Daniel Thayer."

"Tell me about him."

"He owns a lot of businesses and buildings in town," she said. "Some people think he's richer than Big Al. Others don't agree."

"Well, I guess I can talk to Big Al about that, too," Clint said. "Maybe the judge and Thayer arranged to have Jason framed for murder."

"If you can prove that," she said, "we'd be able to get rid of both of them."

"Probably."

"They won't go easy, Mr. Adams."

"Call me Clint." He stood up. "Thank you for the tea and cookies, and for your cooperation."

She also stood. She was tall, young, blond, very pretty—and in mourning.

"Do you think the sheriff would let me see Jason?" she asked. "I'd like to . . . apologize to him."

"I'm sure he would."

"I should also talk to the judge—"

"No," Clint said, "don't do that."

"Why not?"

"I'd like the judge to believe that you still blame Jason for your father's murder," Clint said.

"Oh . . . well, all right."

"Go by the jail later today," he said. "I'll try to arrange for you to see Jason."

"All right."

"Can I go out this way?" he asked, pointing to the door that led to the outside staircase.

"Of course."

He walked to the door and opened it.

"Clint, you should know one more thing."

"What's that?" he asked, turning back.

"Daniel Thayer has been trying to buy my father's store for months."

"And your father wouldn't sell?"

"No, he wouldn't."

"You're right, Beth," he said. "That is something I should know."

TWENTY-FOUR

Clint went directly to Milty's for a beer. He also wanted a conversation with Randy, the bartender.

"Beer?" Randy asked as Clint appeared at the bar.

"Definitely."

Clint looked around, It was early, and there were only a few other patrons in the place. That suited him.

"What brings you in so early?" Randy asked.

"You," Clint said after a healthy sip of cold beer.

Randy frowned.

"What about me?"

"You know everybody in town, don't you?"

"Pretty much, I guess."

"You willing to talk about them?"

Randy frowned again.

"Some," he said.

"Big Al?"

"Sure."

"Daniel Thayer?"

Randy hesitated.

"He doesn't own this place, does he?"

"Naw, I own it," Randy said. "Not that he ain't tried to buy it, though."

"So you'll talk about him?"

"Sure."

"And how about Judge Miller?"

"Is this about the Collins killin'?" Randy asked.

"It is."

"Why are you interested?"

"Big Al asked me to look into it," Clint said. "He thinks his son is innocent."

"You a detective now?"

"Something like that."

Randy looked around, then leaned on the bar.

"Okay, go ahead."

"I hear Collins was on the town council with these other fellows," Clint said.

"That's right."

"You think any of them would have a reason to kill him? Something that has to do with the council?"

"Well, not Big Al."

"Why not?"

"They was always votin' together on the same side," Randy told him.

"What about Thayer and the judge?"

"Now they was always votin' together against Big Al and Ed Collins."

"Was there anything important enough to kill for?" Clint asked. "Maybe now that Collins is dead, they think they can get the vote through?"

"Well," Randy said, "I ain't never sat in on a meeting, ya understand."

"I get it."

"Thayer's always tryin' to buy up more property."

"Like this place?"

"Best saloon in town, figures he'd try to buy it."

"And the mercantile?"

"Yeah, I heard he was tryin' to buy Ed's place."

"What else?"

"Different pieces of property around town," Randy said. He laughed. "He wanted to pull down the old church and build somethin' there."

"What happened?"

"Big Al and Collins blocked him."

"So maybe now he can do it."

"That would depend."

"On what?"

"Not what," Randy said, "who. Depends on who replaces Ed Collins on the council."

"And who do you think might do that?"

"Well, there's a few choices."

"Like who?"

"A couple of businessmen in town," Randy said. "And oh, by the way . . . me."

TWENTY-FIVE

Clint got the names of the two other members of the town council and decided to interview them first. In each case, when he told them he was working for Big Al, they cooperated. Yes, Big Al and Thayer were always at odds at the meetings. Yes, Collins sided with Big Al, and Judge Miller sided with Thayer. When asked who they sided with, both men said it depended on the issue. Both men ran successful businesses—one a hotel, the other a large hardware store—and neither of them seemed particularly afraid of Big Al, Thayer, or the judge.

When asked if they thought either Thayer or the judge would have Ed Collins killed in order to get their way, both men said, "Definitely."

When Clint asked them who was going to replace Collins on the council, they both said a meeting to discuss that had been scheduled for the next day.

Clint thanked both men and left, fairly certain neither had a dog in this fight. However, he was no clearer of whether or not Thayer or the judge was behind Collins's murder.

He went to Big Al Henry's hotel, found the man seated in the large lobby in an overstuffed chair, reading a newspaper. When Henry saw Clint approaching, he closed the newspaper and stood up.

"Do you have something for me yet?" he asked anxiously.

"Yes," Clint said, "more questions."

"Have a seat, then."

They both sat, Clint occupying a twin of Big Al Henry's chair. It was extremely comfortable.

"Here are my suspects," Clint said. "Thayer or the judge, or perhaps one of the men who is in the running to replace Collins on the council."

"You think somebody killed Collins for his seat?" Big Al shook his head. "I don't see it."

"Okay, then who had more to gain from Collins's death, Thayer or the judge?"

"Thayer," Big Al said with no hesitation. "He wanted Ed's business, and he needed Ed's vote."

"So he'll get the vote from whoever replaces Collins on the council."

"Maybe."

"And will he get Collins's business?"

"I'm sure he'll make Beth a generous offer," Henry said.

"And what will she do?"

"I don't know," Henry admitted. "Since her dad died for it, maybe she'll want to keep it. On the other hand, maybe because he died inside, she'll want to get rid of it."

"Okay, what about hired killers?"

"What about them?"

"Does Thayer have anybody working for him who would do the job?" Clint asked.

"Who knows?" Henry said. "If he doesn't, he could always bring somebody in. He's got that kind of money."

"And the judge?"

"He's got some men in town who do dirty jobs for him, but no murder," Henry said.

"Does he have the kind of money it would take to hire it done?" Clint asked.

"He does," Henry said, "but he wouldn't need it. He has that kind of influence."

"Look," Clint said, "I've run into crooked rich men and crooked judges before. It usually helps to bring in some Federal help."

"If you've dealt with men like this before, then you know they have their own influence. Even on a Federal level."

Big Al was careful to say men like "them," ignoring the fact that he was one of these men, as well.

Clint decided to broach the subject.

"Do you have that kind of Federal influence?"

"I have some," Big Al said without bristling. "I'd hardly kill a man and frame my own son, though. Besides, Ed always voted with me on issues."

"So I heard. Who do you think will replace Ed?"

"My best guess? The saloon owner, Randy Kenon."

This was the first time Clint had heard Randy's last name. It meant nothing to him.

"Do you think he'd kill for it?"

"No," Big Al said without hesitation.

"What makes you so sure?"

"I know Randy well," Henry said. "He likes my boy

and Jason likes him. And the reason I think he'll get the seat is that he doesn't care if he gets it."

"I see."

"Have you spoken with Beth?"

"Yes."

"Did she give you any inkling of what she intended to do with the store?"

"No."

"Does she still think Jason killed her father?"

"Actually, no. She listened to what I had to say, and she realized she made an error. She wants to get in to talk with your boy."

"What do you think of that?"

"I see no harm," Clint said. "I'm on my way to talk to Brown about letting her in."

"Why was she so sure Jason did it? The judge?"

"Yes."

"He's not going to be happy that you changed her mind."

"I'm going to talk to him—and to Thayer—after I see the sheriff," Clint said.

Henry grinned and said, "They won't be happy to learn that you're working for me either."

"That's okay with me," Clint said. "I'm not particularly concerned about making them happy."

TWENTY-SIX

"She wants to what?" Brown asked. He obviously wasn't sure he'd heard Clint correctly.

"She wants to talk to Jason."

"But why?"

"She no longer thinks he killed her father."

Brown sat back in his chair.

"You accomplished that already?" he asked. "You changed her mind?"

"I just told her what I knew," Clint said. "She made up her own mind, On the other hand, she hadn't made up her own mind before. The judge had."

"He's not gonna be happy."

"We'll see," Clint said. "I'm going to talk to him when I'm done here. Will you let her in?"

"Sure," Brown said, "but I'll have to search her for a gun. I'm not so sure she's changed her mind."

"You'll see," Clint said. "Try not to enjoy searching her too much, though."

"I'm a professional, Adams," Sheriff Brown said.

Clint started for the door and said, "I'm depending on that, Sheriff."

Clint was able to convince the judge's male clerk that he should announce him to the man. The clerk came out of the judge's office and said, "This way."

He followed the clerk into the judge's office. The last time he'd done this, he'd encountered a man so fat he couldn't get up from his desk. This judge, however, though portly, stood up to greet him. Also, there was no food on his desk.

"Mr. Adams," the judge said, "what a pleasure." He might have thought it was a pleasure—or not—but he didn't offer to shake hands. "Have a seat, please."

Clint sat in a hard wooden chair across from the judge. The man was in his sixties, but seemed to have a vitality that belied his years and showed in his bright, clear blue eyes.

"Tell me, what brings you here?" Miller asked, taking his seat again.

"Big Al Henry."

The judge frowned.

"What about him?"

"He's hired me."

"Big Al has hired a gunman?"

"No," Clint said, shaking his head, "not my gun."

"What then?"

"He's hired me to prove that his son didn't kill Ed Collins," Clint said.

He watched the man's face closely. The judge was good. He played his emotions close to the vest. He had an excellent poker face.

"And why would he do that?" Judge Miller asked. "The boy is guilty."

"He doesn't think so."

"And he's paying you to prove it?" Miller asked. "He's wasting his money, and you're taking it under false pretenses."

"I don't think so, Judge," Clint said. "From everything I've learned so far, I don't think the boy did it."

"You rode into town when? Yesterday?"

"That's right."

"And you think you know the boy that well?"

"I've been asking questions," Clint said, "so yes, I'm pretty sure he's innocent."

"Well, if you feel that way, then you must have some idea who's guilty."

"I have some ideas."

"Like who?"

"Well, there are some members of the town council who might have hired it done. When the boy walked in on the deed, the killers decided to frame him."

"Wait, wait, go back," the judge said. "Somebody on the council? You mean . . . like me?"

"You're on my list."

Miller stared at Clint, then slapped his pudgy hand down on his desktop with a loud bang.

"By God, man, you've got gall!"

"Maybe you," Clint went on, "maybe Daniel Thayer."

"Thayer is an upstanding citizen of this town," Miller said. "And may I remind you of my own title?"

"I know who you are, Judge," Clint said. "I also know that you and Thayer vote together on the council, and were often opposed by Big Al Henry . . . and Ed Collins."

"If that's the case," Miller said, "then why isn't Big Al Henry dead?"

"Well, that would be a little harder to explain," Clint said. "The murder of one of the wealthiest men in the county? Daniel Thayer would go right to the top of that suspect list, with you a close second."

"More and more gall," Miller said.

"Of course," Clint said, "there are others . . . also, I'm sure you or Thayer would hire it done. I just have to find the men—or women—who did it and ask them who hired them."

"Women?"

"Well," Clint said, "maybe one woman."

"You think a woman killed Collins?"

Clint spread his hands.

"I'm just saying it could be anyone," Clint said. "But I'll find them, and then we'll know who they work for."

"I think we're done here, sir," the judge said.

"So do I, Judge," Clint said, getting to his feet, "so do I. Have a good day."

TWENTY-SEVEN

Clint was surprised to find that Daniel Thayer did not have an office in town, and lived in a modest house just inside the town limits.

He knocked on the door. Normally, he would have expected a man who owned half a town to have a servant answer the door. A tall, broad-shouldered man in his fifties but in good physical shape answered.

"Can I help you?" the man asked.

"I'm looking for Daniel Thayer."

"You found him."

"Oh. I thought . . . I didn't expect you to answer your own door," Clint said.

Thayer smiled. It was disarming.

"And I bet you expected some huge house with four white columns," he said.

"Something like that."

"Well, the reason I'm as rich as I am is that I don't indiscriminately spend money. And you are?"

"My name is Clint Adams."

"The Gunsmith!" Thayer looked very pleased. "What a pleasure. Come in, please."

Clint entered and Thayer closed the door.

"Please, in here."

He led Clint to a small but well-appointed living room. Clint could smell something cooking.

"Something smells good," Clint said. "Do you cook?"

"No," Thayer said, "I may not have servants, but a cook is absolutely necessary. I'd probably burn down the house. Can I offer you something? Coffee? Brandy?"

"Coffee would be good," Clint said. He was off balance. This wasn't the type of man he was expecting.

"Have a seat."

Thayer went into the kitchen. Clint heard him have a short conversation with a woman, then the man reappeared with a cup of coffee in each hand. He handed one to Clint.

"If you want cream or sugar—"

"No, just black is fine."

"That's the way I take it." Thayer sat down on the sofa. Clint sat in an armchair with studs in the arms and down the legs.

"So tell, Mr. Adams," Thayer said, "what brings you to Copper Canyon—and more specifically, what brings you to my door?"

"Well, as for Copper Canyon, I'm really just passing through," Clint said. "I happened to arrive yesterday, when that murder happened."

"Yes, Ed Collins," Thayer said. "A good friend of mine. I'm so sorry—and that poor boy who did it. He's very disturbed, but I never thought he was a killer."

"Well, the fact is," Clint said, "his father has hired me to prove that he isn't."

Thayer frowned.

"I see. And why does that bring you to me?"

"Well, you sat on the town council with Ed Collins."

"That's right."

"And forgive me, but from everything I've heard, you weren't particularly friendly."

Thayer sat forward, set his coffee cup down on the table in front of the sofa.

"I don't know who you've been talking to," Thayer said. "I know Ed and I were on opposite sides of some issues, but that doesn't mean we weren't friends."

"I understand you were also trying to buy his store."

"That was just business," Thayer said. "Listen, what's the point of these questions?"

"I'm just wondering what motive, if any, you might have had to have Collins killed."

Thayer hesitated a moment, then said, "What?"

"I said—"

"I heard what you said." The man stood and drew himself up to his full height. "I think you better leave."

"No, Mr. Thayer," Clint said, "there's no reason to get upset. You've got to admit that you make a likely suspect for Ed Collins's death. You and the judge, that is."

"Judge Miller?" Thayer said. "Did you accuse him, as well. I can't imagine he stood for that."

"I didn't accuse him," Clint said, "and I'm not accusing you. I'm just asking questions."

"Questions I don't like."

"Why don't you have a seat?" Clint said. "Go on, sit

back down. I only have a few other questions. Besides, this coffee is excellent, and I'd like to finish it."

Thayer looked undecided about what to do, then finally sat back down.

"You're a rich man, Mr. Thayer, as you yourself have said," Clint said. "You must have a lot of different types of people working for you."

"Whoa, hold on!" Thayer said. "I can tell where you're heading now. I do not have hired killers on my payroll and I resent your implying that I do."

"Again, I'm not implying or accusing," Clint said. "I'm asking."

"The answer is no," Thayer said. "I do not have any hired killers working for me."

"Well, that's good," Clint said, putting his empty coffee cup down on the table.

"And I think you really better leave now," Thayer said, although he didn't stand.

"Well, sure," Clint said, "I'll leave now."

They both stood up.

"I'm sorry if you were offended by my questions, Mr. Thayer," Clint said, "but I'm going to find out who killed Collins, and who hired them to do it."

"You're so sure the boy didn't do it?"

"I have no doubt about his innocence," Clint said. "Thanks for your time."

Clint left the man standing in the middle of his living room.

TWENTY-EIGHT

Thayer was good.

If his indignant manner was an act, the man was worthy
of a stage career. But Clint didn't believe it for a minute.
You didn't get to where Thayer was in his life without
knowing how to play people.

Clint walked back toward the center of town. The thing
that was sticking in his mind after spending half the day
asking questions was the smell Jason had talked about.
The smell of a sweet soap. Letty had smelled fresh and
clean when she came to his room the night before. Beth
had smelled good, obviously having bathed that morning.
But neither girl smelled particular sweet. Clint felt there
had to have been a woman in that back room, unless there
was a very sweet-smelling man someplace in Copper
Canyon.

And he couldn't very well go around town sniffing all
the men.

* * *

Stephanie Kitten came out of the kitchen after Clint Adams left the house.

"That was close," she said.

"He's got a lot of damned nerve talking to me that way!" Daniel Thayer blustered.

"He's the Gunsmith, Daniel," Stephanie said. "He can talk any way he wants as long as he backs it up with his gun. I notice you were real cooperative with him."

"I had to act innocent," Thayer said. "Say, your two idiot partners aren't outside, are they?"

"No," she said, "don't worry. When I came over here, I left them behind."

Thayer turned and looked at her. She had showed up at his door just minutes before the Gunsmith. It was a close thing. He had just let her in the back door when Adams knocked on the front.

"I don't think your cook approves of women wearin' guns," Stephanie said. "She was givin' me dirty looks the whole time I was in the kitchen."

"Mrs. Marcus believes women belong in the kitchen."

"Well, not this woman."

"Look," Thayer said, "if I need you and your partners to take care of Adams, can you do it?"

"Of course we can do it," Stephanie said, "but it ain't gonna come cheap."

"I didn't think so." He turned to face her. "Why did you come here in the first place?"

"Because Adams has been around town asking questions," she said. "I wanted to know if he'd been here." "Well, now you know," Thayer said. "He talked to me and Miller."

"And he sounds determined to find out who killed the storekeeper."

"And if he does?" Thayer asked. "Are you going to tell him who paid you?"

"I don't know," she said.

"What do you mean, you don't know?"

"I guess that would depend on how much you pay me not to tell him."

When Clint reached his hotel, he did not go in. He also decided not to go to Milty's Saloon. He'd been asking questions all afternoon, and he was hungry. But he didn't want to eat in his hotel dining room, in case somebody came looking for him. He kept walking until he found a small café to go into.

He sat at a back table, the place almost full as people came in for their supper. He saw a couple of steaks on other tables, but decided against trying one. Instead, he ordered a bowl of beef stew.

Drinking coffee while he waited for his food, he studied the men and women around him—some with children of varying ages—but he couldn't smell anything sweet on any of them. He wondered if what Jason had smelled might not be soap, after all. Maybe some kind of lilac water, or actual candy? Someone in that back room could have been eating something sweet. If that was what it was—and not soap—it would be ever harder to identify.

The waiter brought his beef stew along with a basket of biscuits. It was hot, not very tasty, but filling enough to do the trick. He continued to watch as people came and went, some of them glancing at him, others not paying him any mind, at all—all of which suited him fine.

* * *

Stephanie Kitten found her two partners where she thought she'd find them, in Andy Choate's mother's café.

"You don't look happy," Tony Black said.

"You're wrong," she said, sitting down. "I'm very happy."

"About what?" Choate asked.

"Thayer is gonna pay us a lot of money."

Both men looked dubious.

"To do what?" Choate asked.

She looked around to make sure nobody was close enough to hear them.

"Clint Adams is askin' too many questions," she said. "Thayer doesn't want him findin' us."

"Why would the Gunsmith find us?" Andy asked nervously.

"Because he's lookin'," Stephanie said. "Big Al hired Adams to prove his boy is innocent."

"That's not good," Black said.

"Yeah, it is, Tony," Stephanie corrected him.

"Whataya mean?" Choate asked.

"I told you," Stephanie said with great patience. "Thayer is gonna pay us a lot of money to take care of the Gunsmith."

"Oh, I don't like the sound of that," Andy said.

"Don't do that to me, Andy," Stephanie said. "We're in this together."

"Okay," Andy said, "how much money are we talkin' about?"

TWENTY-NINE

After he'd finished eating, Clint stopped at the sheriff's office to see if Beth had been there yet. As he walked in, Deputy Ott was coming out of the cell block. Sheriff Brown was seated behind his desk.

"Just gave your boy some supper," Brown said.

"Has Beth come by yet?" Clint asked.

"She was here," Brown said with a nod. "Spent about five minutes back there with him."

"Good," Clint said. He removed his gun and set it on the desktop. "I'll just need a minute."

"Sure."

"I'm gonna go get some supper, Sheriff," the deputy said as Clint entered the cell block.

"Bring something back for me," Brown said.

Clint walked in, saw Jason Henry sitting on his cot, eating his supper.

"Heard you had a visitor today," Clint said.

Jason looked up and grinned.

"Miss Beth came in," he said. "She says she knows I didn't kill her father."

"That's good."

"Can't they let me out now?"

"I'm sorry, Jason," Clint said, "it doesn't work that way."

"Then when can I go home?"

"As soon as I can prove that somebody else killed Mr. Collins," Clint explained.

"Like who?" Jason asked.

"That's what I'm trying to find out."

"Well," Jason said, "I'm glad Miss Beth forgives me."

"There's nothing to forgive, Jason," Clint said. "She doesn't believe you killed her father."

"She's nice," Jason said.

"Yeah, she is," Clint said. "Okay, you finish your supper."

Jason nodded and went back to eating.

Clint went out to the sheriff's desk and reclaimed his gun, slid it back into his holster.

"Has the judge set a trial date?" he asked.

"As soon as he collects a jury," Brown said.

"That could take days."

"Normally."

"Meaning?"

"When the judge wants a jury—a cooperative jury—he usually gets one pretty quick."

"Meaning he handpicks them?"

Brown nodded.

"Jesus."

"You got any ideas?"

"Both Thayer and the judge had motive," Clint said, "to hire the killing done."

"Motive?"

"Profit."

Brown nodded.

"Always a good motive."

"So they would have had it done," Clint said. "The question is by who?"

"Can I speak frankly?" Brown asked.

"Sure," Clint said, "I'd prefer it."

"Normally," Brown said, "I'd think maybe that's why *you* were here."

"Really?"

"Well, your reputation, and all."

"I just got here yesterday."

"And Collins was killed yesterday."

"Good point."

Brown shrugged and said, "I'm just saying."

"No, I can see how you might think that."

"It's my job."

"And as part of your job," Clint asked, "are you looking into Thayer and the judge, too?"

"I'm keeping an open mind."

Clint nodded.

"Got any more questions for me?"

"No," Brown said, "I don't actually suspect you. Although it would be funny."

"What would?"

"If you were hired to look into a killing you committed."

"Yeah," Clint said, "that would be funny, wouldn't it?"

THIRTY

Clint left the sheriff's office. The man had not offended him. It made sense to consider him a suspect. He arrived in town, and a man was killed. Of course, it helped that he was in the saloon when the shots were heard. Randy was his witness.

And although Randy was up for Ed Collins's spot on the council, Clint was his witness. He was behind the bar when the shooting occurred. Unless he had hired it done.

Everything pointed to the killing being hired out. Jason stumbled into it, but it wouldn't hurt Thayer or the judge if they could hang the murder on Big Al's son.

So he had to find any hired killers who were in town, or had been in town at the time of the killing. Unless, of course, they rode in, did it, and rode out. But more often than not, a hired killer came in and got the lay of the land before doing the job.

He had to check all the hotels and rooming houses, see if anyone had checked in a day or two before the killing, and had either checked out right after or was still in residence.

He decided to start with his own hotel . . .

The desk clerk allowed him to look at the register book. Two men had checked in a couple of days before, along with a man and a woman.

"A married couple, I think," the clerk said.

"And are they still here?"

"Well, these two men checked out the day before the murder," the clerk said, "but these two—the man and the woman—they're still here."

Clint looked at their room number. It was several doors down from his.

"Are they in their rooms now?"

"I don't think so. I think they went out."

"Together?"

The clerk shook his head.

"Separate."

"What do they look like?"

The clerk, a young man, didn't have the words to properly describe the man.

"He's tall, dark-haired, dressed like a salesman."

"Is he a salesman?"

"I don't know."

"And her?"

Now his face softened.

"She's pretty," he said, "real pretty."

"How old?"

"I think they're—he's older, in his thirties, but she looks like she's still in her twenties."

"Like you?"

"No," he said, "I'm twenty-four. She was older."

"And how did she smell?"

"Smell?"

"Yeah," Clint said, "how did she smell?"

The clerk thought a moment, then said, "She smells good, I guess."

"Sweet?"

"What?"

"Did she smell particularly sweet?"

"No."

"Okay," Clint said, "thanks."

As he turned to walk to the door, the clerk said, "But he did."

"What?" Clint turned.

"The man," the clerk said. "He smelled sweet."

"Did he?"

"Yeah," the clerk said. "I thought it was . . . odd. You know, a man smelling like that."

"Yeah," Clint said, "odd. Uh, what are their names again?"

The clerk looked at the book.

"He's Henry Wilkins, and she's . . . Amanda Kyle."

"Different names, but you thought they were married?"

The young man shrugged.

"I didn't read their names right away," he said, "but they acted like they were married."

"Okay," Clint said. He just had to find the sweet-smelling man, Henry Wilkins, and ask him some questions.

He started out toward the door, then stopped again.

"How much luggage did they have?"

"Quite a few bags," the clerk said. "You know, he's probably a . . . a drummer of some kind. Some of them looked like sample cases, you know?"

"Yes," Clint said, "I do know."

"What are you thinking?" Sheriff Brown asked.

"That maybe Wilkins and the woman, Kyle, came to town to do the killing. They checked into the hotel, but they didn't check out after the job was done. That would be too suspicious."

"Could be."

"Did you ever see them?" Clint asked. "This drummer and his maybe wife?"

"No, I don't think so. I mean, I don't keep track of every traveling salesman who comes to town."

"That might've been what they were counting on."

"Damn," Brown said, sitting back in his chair.

"And the man," Clint said, "the desk clerk says he smelled . . . sweet."

"A man? Smelling that way? Why?"

"I don't know," Clint said. "Let's find him, and maybe we'll find out."

THIRTY-ONE

They left the office together, but then split up, both looking for the sweet-smelling drummer, or his maybe wife.

"If you find him," Brown said, "bring him back here. We'll question him together."

"Agreed."

As they split up, Clint found himself heading toward Milty's, so he thought he'd start there. It would make sense for a salesman—a real salesman—to spend some time there.

"Can't stay away, eh?" Randy asked. The place was in full swing, with all the gaming tables open and the girls working the floor.

"Have you seen a drummer in town?" Clint asked.

"Seen lots of drummers in town," Randy said.

"This one's got a pretty woman with him," Clint said, "smells kind of sweet."

"She does? I ain't had a sweet-smellin' woman in here in a while. All these girls wear cheap stuff."

"No, not the woman," Clint said. "The man smells sweet."

"Oh? Well, I sure ain't seen a sweet-smellin' man in here . . . ever!"

"Okay, thanks."

"Beer?"

"No, I've got to find these people."

"Check the dress shops and hat shops and such for the girl," Randy suggested.

"Good point," Clint said. "Thanks."

He left the saloon and walked to Beth Collins's store. Inside he found himself buffeted on all sides by women. He inhaled, though, and found none of them particularly sweet smelling.

"Clint!" Beth waved from behind the counter, then pointed toward the back of the store.

"Don't you need to be behind the counter?" he asked when they met at the back.

"I have help today," she said. "In fact, I've been trying to close for the past half hour, but I've been too busy. What brings you here?"

He told her who he was looking for, asked if she'd seen either of them in his store.

"I might have," she said. "A couple did come in—wait, he was carrying a drummer's case. And he smelled kind of sweet."

"When was that?"

"A couple of hours ago, I guess."

"Did you hear them say anything to each other about where they were going?"

"No, I'm afraid not."

"And why were they here?"

"She bought some buttons."

"Buttons?"

She nodded.

"That was it?"

"I'm afraid so. Who are they?" Then her eyes went wide and she covered her mouth with both hands. "You think they're the ones who killed my father?"

"I don't know, Beth," he said. "Right now the sheriff and I are just trying to find them to ask them a few questions."

"Oh my God . . ."

He took her by the shoulders and said, "Just go back to work. I'll talk to you later. Will you be home?"

"Yes," she said, "I'm just going to make myself a small dinner. There will be enough for two, if you like."

"That would be great," Clint said. "I haven't had a home-cooked meal in some time."

"Good," she said. "I'll expect you."

"What time?"

"Come by when you can," she said. "I'll keep it hot."

"All right," he said.

He turned to leave but she reached out and grabbed his sleeve.

"Be careful," she said. "If they are the killers—just be very careful."

"I'm always careful," he said.

He left and she waded back in among her customers.

"Why ain't we out followin' Clint Adams?" Tony Black asked Stephanie.

Stephanie stared at him. Andy was in the kitchen with his mother for some reason.

"Tony, this is the Gunsmith we're talkin' about," she said. "Don't you think he'd know if he was bein' followed?"

"I guess."

"We'll get our chance."

"Not sittin' here, we won't," he complained. "I've had enough coffee to last me a month."

"Mary's coffee is the best in town," she said. "Don't let her hear you complainin'."

"Ah—" he started, but Andy returned, carrying a basket full of buns his mom had just finished making. While her food was only fair, her baking was the best in town.

"Dig in!" Andy said.

Tony took one and absently nibbled on it.

"What's wrong with him?"

"He's gettin' impatient."

"Relax, Tony," Andy said. "Steph always picks the right time."

"You tell him, Andy."

Andy beamed. He enjoyed any praise he could get from Stephanie Kitten.

"Yeah, yeah . . ." Tony said.

"In fact, you boys enjoy the buns," she said, standing. "I'm just gonna check around town a bit. And I wanna find that drummer."

"What for?" Andy asked.

"I wanna buy some more of his soap," she said. "I really like it."

She held her hand out and Andy sniffed it.

"Sure smells sweet," he said.

THIRTY-TWO

Clint continued to comb his part of town for the drummer and his lady. It was getting dark and he was about to quit and go back to the jail to see if the sheriff had had any luck when he saw a group of women assembled.

He moved to the back of the assembly until he could see what they were interested in. The drummer had set his case up on a stand and had opened it. His assistant, a pretty woman, was passing out samples to the women.

And there was a sweet, sweet scent in the air.

"Here you go, ladies," the drummer said. "Sniff what my assistant is giving you. Those are samples, but the real thing ain't expensive at all. What's it worth to you to smell sweet?"

Clint allowed the man to finish making his pitch, then whatever sales he could, and then the women dispersed. One woman, however, didn't go far.

"What about you, sir?" the drummer asked. "Didn't see

you back there. Would you like to buy some for your lady friend?"

"Afraid not," Clint said. "Is your name Henry Wilkins?"

"Why, yes it is."

"And you're Amanda Kyle?"

"I am," the pretty girl said. She and Wilkins exchanged curious glances.

"Well, I'll need you both to come with me to the sheriff's office."

"What for?" Wilkins asked.

"The sheriff would like to talk to you."

Wilkins frowned.

"Are you a deputy?"

"I'm not," Clint said. "I'm just trying to help the sheriff with something."

"I don't know . . ." Kyle said.

"What's this about?" Wilkins asked.

"Murder," Clint said.

"What?"

"Don't put your hand in that case, Mr. Wilkins."

"What?" the drummer asked again, looking astonished. He pulled his hand out of the case. "You think I have a gun in there?"

"I don't know what you have in there," Clint said with his hand hovering above his gun. "It would just be smart for you to keep your hands where I can see them."

"Soap!" Wilkins asked.

"What?"

"I sell soap," Wilkins said. "The case is filled with soap. Sweet-smelling soap."

Which would explain why the air was so sweet smelling.

"All right," Clint said, "let's close the case and take a walk to the sheriff's office, shall we?"

Stephanie Kitten stood off to one side, holding the three bars of soap she had just bought from the drummer. She watched Clint Adams walk the man and woman away, taking them to the sheriff's office, and she thought she knew what he was thinking.

He thought the drummer and his gal had killed Ed Collins. She had to admit, hiding behind the guise of a drummer would be a good idea for a hired killer. Only she happened to know that wasn't the case.

Once Adams got them to the sheriff's office and he and Sheriff Brown questioned them, they'd realize they'd made a mistake. And they'd be real frustrated.

Stephanie waited until they were out of sight, then turned and headed back to Mary Choate's café.

"This is preposterous," Henry Wilkins said as they entered the sheriff's office.

"Just keep walking," Clint said.

"You found 'em," Brown said, getting up from his desk. Ott was standing by the stove with a cup of coffee.

"I did," Clint said. "Sheriff, this is Amanda Kyle, and this is Henry Wilkins. Mr. Wilkins is a drummer. He sells . . . soap."

"Soap?"

"That's right."

Brown sniffed the air and said, "That must be why he smells so sweet."

"That's not me," Wilkins said. "It's the soap you smell. People often make that mistake."

"Have a seat, folks," Brown said. "Mr. Adams and I are going to slip out to have a talk, but my deputy will be right here."

They both turned to look at Ott.

"Don't let them leave, Kenny," Brown said.

"No sir."

"Clint?"

Clint accompanied the sheriff into the cell block.

"What's going on?" Jason asked.

"In a minute, son," Brown said. He looked at Clint. "Soap?"

"I know," Clint said. "If he's been selling it around town—"

"A lot of folks could be smelling sweet," Brown finished for him.

"A lot of women," Clint said.

"So we're still looking for a woman," Sheriff Brown said, "just maybe not this one."

"Maybe not," Clint said. "Let's talk to them, but I'm inclined to believe I may have made a mistake."

"Don't be so quick to judge," Brown said. "Let's see what they have to say for themselves first."

"Okay," Clint said.

They went back into the office.

After twenty minutes of questioning the couple, Sheriff Brown was inclined to agree with Clint Adams. These folks were not hired killers disguised as drummers.

"Can we go now?" Wilkins demanded. He started to get braver as he realized what was happening.

"In a minute," Clint said. He signaled to Brown to join him in the cell block.

"What?" Brown asked. "We've got to let them go."

"I know," Clint said, "but first let's find out how many different kinds of soap they've got."

"You wanna buy soap?"

"No," Clint said, "but I want Jason to smell them and see if he can pick out the one he smelled in the store."

Brown rubbed his jaw.

"Okay," he said, "identifying that scent might come in handy."

Clint nodded and they went back into the office.

"Mr. Wilkins," Brown asked, "how many different soap smells do you have in that case?"

"We sell six distinctly different scents," the drummer said, drawing himself up proudly.

"I see." Brown and Clint exchanged a glance. It could have been worse.

"Sir," Brown said, "there's something we'd like to do before we let you and your assistant go—with our apologies, of course."

Suspiciously, Wilkins asked. "And what's that?"

THIRTY-THREE

Armed with six bars of soap, Clint reentered the cell block.

"What's happening?" Jason asked, starting to rise.

"Stay where you are, Jason," Clint said. He put five of the bars of soap down on the floor, away from the cell.

"Whataya got?"

"I've got some bars of soap," Clint told him. "I want you to smell each one, and tell me which one you smelled in Mr. Collins's store—if any."

"But why?"

"Just do it, okay?"

"Okay, Mr. Adams."

"All right, come to the front of the cell."

Jason did as he was told.

"I'll hold it, and you smell it."

"Okay."

Clint held the first bar of soap up, and Jason sniffed at it.

"Anything?" Clint asked.

"No."

"Okay."

Clint walked to the little pile of soap bars he'd left on the floor, put the first one down, picked up a second, and walked back to the cell door.

"Smell this one."

Jason did, and said, "No."

Clint repeated the routine with a third and a fourth bar of soap, only to have Jason shake his head two more times. Clint was starting to think this exercise was going to be fruitless when he took the fifth bar of soap over to the boy.

When Jason sniffed that fifth bar, he said, "That's it. That's what I smelled."

"Are you sure?"

"Yessir."

"Smell it again."

Jason did, and he nodded his head vigorously.

"That's it."

Clint looked down at the bar of soap in his hand.

"Okay, kid," Clint said. "Sit back and relax."

Clint picked up the soaps and carried them out with him. He put five of them back into the drummer's case.

"This is the one," Clint said, holding up the bar of soap in a pale blue wrapper. "What kind is this?"

"It's called Rosebud."

"Okay," Clint said, "this is the soap the killer smelled like."

"You can go," Sheriff Brown said to Henry Wilkins and Amanda Kyle.

"Come on, Henry," Amanda said, "before they change their mind."

Wilkins started to close his case, then stopped.

"What about my soap?" he asked.

"We need this bar as evidence," Brown said.

"It's a nickel," Wilkins said.

"Are you kiddin'?" Ott asked.

"No," Wilkins said.

"Mr. Wilkins—" Brown started.

"Never mind," Clint said. "I'll give him the nickel."

"A nickel for soap?" Ott demanded.

"You kept me here 'til after dark," Wilkins said. "I can't make any more sales today."

"Here you go," Clint said, handing over a nickel. Then something occurred to me. "Say, Wilkins, do you remember how many bars of this soap you sold?"

"I can look," Wilkins said. "I know how many we had when we got here."

"Would you do that, please?" Clint asked.

Amanda was waiting impatiently by the door.

Wilkins looked into his case, started counting.

"Four," he said. "Looks like I sold four."

"That's all?" Brown asked.

"Sold more Lilac than anything else," the drummer said. "Also the Springtime scent."

"Did you sell the four bars to four different women?" Clint asked.

"I don't remember."

"I do," Amanda said from the door.

"You do?" Wilkins asked.

She nodded.

"Sold all four to the same woman," she said. "She bought one bar when we first got to town, then bought three more just today."

"When?" Clint asked.

"Well," Amanda said, "she was there when you came and got us."

"In that band of women?" Clint asked.

Amanda nodded.

"Do you remember what she looked like?"

"Real pretty," Amanda said, "tall, blond, and . . . oh, she was wearing a gun and holster."

"A woman wearing a gun?" Wilkins asked. "Hey, yeah, I remember her now."

Clint looked at Sheriff Brown.

"You know a woman like that in town? Pretty blonde who wears a gun?"

"Gotta be Stephanie," Brown said. "Stephanie Kitten."

"Kitten?" Amanda asked with a grin. "Is that really her last name?"

"That's it," Brown said.

"Where does she live?" Clint asked.

"Used to live in a small house outside of town," Brown said.

"She work with anybody?" Clint asked. "A man?"

"Two men," Brown said. "Fella she grew up with, Tony Black, and a friend of theirs, Andy Choate."

"Do you know where they live now?"

"No," Brown said, "but Choate's mother owns a small, run-down café."

"Well then," Clint said, "maybe we should go and get something to eat."

THIRTY-FOUR

Sheriff Brown showed Clint the way to Mary Choate's café, which had no name on the window or above the door. Like he said, it was a run-down café in a falling-down part of town. As they entered, there were a few people there. Clint doubted the place was ever overcrowded.

"Let's have a seat," Clint suggested.

"Don't order a meal," Brown warned. "Mary's not a very good cook, but she's a helluva baker. Have a piece of pie if you want something."

"I just might do that."

A woman came out of the kitchen, carrying two plates. She was a washed-out middle-aged woman with dark hair that was shot with gray. She set the two plates down on a table, then spotted the sheriff.

"Well, well," she said, coming over, "local law come to call. Who's your handsome friend?"

"This is Clint Adams," Brown said. "I told him what a baker you are and he decided he wanted a piece of pie."

"Ah." She looked at Clint. "Rhubarb or apple?"

"No peach?"

"Not today."

"Apple, then," he said. "Never rhubarb."

"Rhubarb's had its day," she said. "Folks just don't like it anymore. Well, comin' up. Coffee?"

"Sure."

"And you, Sheriff?"

"I'll have the rhubarb, Mary."

"Attaboy," she said, and hurried to the kitchen.

"Seems like you know her pretty well," Clint said. "Not the boy? Andy?"

"No," Brown said, "I never got to know Andy."

"What about Stephanie and the other one, Tony? You're the same age, aren't you?"

"Yeah," Brown said, "but other side of the tracks, you know?"

"Ah."

Mary reappeared, carrying a tray with two slices of pie and two cups of coffee.

"There you go," she said, setting them down.

"Have a seat, Mary," the sheriff said. "Come on, you're not that busy."

She looked around, saw she had no excuse not to, so she sat down with them.

Clint tried a bite of the pie. Brown was right, she was a good baker. The crust was light and flaky, and the apples were sweet.

"Mary," Brown said, "we're looking for Andy and his friends."

"Andy has lots of friends," she said. "Which ones?"

Clint could see that Mary Choate had been a good-looking

woman in her day. In fact, if she did something to fix herself up, she still wouldn't be bad.

"You know which ones," Brown said, "because he only has two—Stephanie Kitten and Tony Black."

"Those two," Mary said.

"What's wrong with them?" Clint asked.

"They boss him around, tell him what to do."

"And he does it?"

"He's smitten with that girl," Mary said. "Always has been. And who can blame him? She's a pretty one."

"And Tony?"

"Handsome lad," she said. "If I was a few years younger . . ."

"Have you seen them?" Brown asked. "Lately?"

"They eat here once in a while," she said, which, Clint noticed, didn't really answer the question.

"Eat here today?" he asked.

"No," she said. "They must have found someplace else."

"Have you noticed anything different about Stephanie these days?" Brown asked.

"Different? Like what?"

"The way she smells maybe?" Clint asked.

"Kinda sweet, is that what you mean?" she asked. "I think she's got a new soap."

"That's what I mean," Clint said. He ate the last hunk of pie. Brown had had a few bites, left the rest, but they both finished their coffee, which was good and strong,

"Why are you lookin' for them?" she asked. "And my boy?"

"I just need to ask them some questions," the sheriff said.

"Got themselves into some trouble?"

"Maybe."

"Kids," she said, shaking her head.

"Mrs. Choate," Clint said, "if you don't mind my saying, you must have been very young when you had Andy."

She smiled. It made her look pretty.

"I was sixteen," she said. "Andy's twenty-six now."

"Younger than Stephanie and Tony?"

"Oh, yes," she said. "They're in their thirties. About fifteen years younger than me, but to me, they're still kids." She fixed Clint with an interested stare and asked, "And how old are you, handsome?"

"Time for us to go, Mary," Brown said, standing up.

She and Clint also stood.

"I don't suppose I can ask you not to tell Andy we were looking for him."

"Why not?" she asked. "I'll just tell him to stop by the jail."

"And he will?" Clint asked.

"Of course," she said. "I'm sure he'd like to help."

"Yeah," Brown said, "I'm sure he will."

"What do I owe you for the pie, ma'am?" Clint asked. "It was very good."

"It's on the house, handsome," she said. "Come back sometime without the law. Maybe we can get better acquainted."

"Good night, Mrs. Choate," Clint said.

"Mary," she said. "You can just call me Mary."

Clint smiled, and he and Brown left.

Mary Choate waited a few moments, to make sure the sheriff and Clint Adams were really gone, and then went back into the kitchen.

"Ma—" Andy said.

She slapped him and his head rocked back from the force of the blow.

"What did you and your friends do now, Andy?" she asked. "Why is the law after you?"

"I don't know, Ma!" he said, holding his cheek. "Honest."

"Don't lie to me, Andy."

"I ain't, Ma."

"Right," she said. "If that girl told you to blow your own head off, you'd do it."

"Ma—"

"Never mind," She said. "Whatever you three idiots did, you better tell those two to lay low."

"I'll tell them."

"And," she said, putting her hand on her son's shoulder, "you tell that Tony Black if he wants to lay low with me, he's welcome."

"Aw, Ma—"

"I know, I know," she said, "he's sweet on Steph, too. But maybe he just needs an older woman to show him how to handle her."

"Aw, Ma . . ." Andy Choate said, looking sick to his stomach.

"Never mind," she said. "Just get out of here, find them, and warn them."

"Yes, Ma."

He started toward the doorway to the dining room and she said, "No, damn it, go out the back!"

THIRTY-FIVE

"She's gonna go right to her son," Brown said as they walked away.

"I know," Clint said. "And then he'll go right to his friends."

"They might leave town."

"Thereby admitting their guilt," Clint said. "Then you'd have to form a posse and go after them."

"The judge wouldn't like that."

"Can he stop you?"

"Not right away," Brown said, "but eventually he can take my badge."

"He'd have to go to the mayor and the town council for that, right?"

"Right."

"Well," Clint said, "if he hired the killers, and we prove it, he won't be able to do that."

"But if he didn't hire them, and we prove that the boy

is innocent, he might still come after me," Brown said. "He wants to put Big Al's son on trial."

"Well," Clint said, "Andy and his friends aren't gone yet."

"No, they're not."

"You know anybody else you can trust other than your deputy?" Clint asked.

"To tell you the truth," the lawman answered, "I don't even know that I can trust him."

"Okay," Clint said, "then I can only think of one other person we can trust not to be working with either the judge or Daniel Thayer."

"Who's that?"

Clint looked at the sheriff and said, "Big Al Henry."

Clint and Sheriff Brown decided that Andy Choate, Stephanie Kitten, and Tony Black were not going to leave town at night.

"Besides," Clint said, "they haven't been hired to run. I think whoever hired them would send them after me before he'd let them leave town."

"So you think they'll come for you tomorrow?"

"Who knows?" Clint said. "But we'll probably find out . . . tomorrow."

So the sheriff went back to his office, while Clint went to have a talk with Big Al . . .

At the hotel he found Big Al Henry in his suite. The man poured them some brandy and they sat and talked.

"Seems you've gotten a lot of work done in a short time," Big Al said.

"Not so short," Clint said. "It's been a long day." Clint sipped his drink.

"What have you found?"

"A sweet-smelling assassin," Clint said.

"What?"

"A lady with a gun who bought some new soap," Clint said. "Your son smelled it when he went into that store."

"A lady with a gun?"

"And two friends."

"Wait," Big Al, "it sounds like you're talking about Stephanie Kitten."

"Come on, now," Clint said, "is that really her name?"

"Her father was Tom Kitten," Big Al said. "He worked for me a long time ago."

"Tell me you parted on good terms."

"Not at all," Big Al said. "I fired him, had him arrested . . . and he hung himself in his cell."

"How long ago was that?"

"Twenty years."

"And she'd hold a grudge that long?"

"Wouldn't you?"

"Is she a killer?"

"Before now," Big Al said, "I would've said no."

"Who would she go to work for?" Clint asked. "Thayer or the judge?"

"Whichever paid her the most money," Big Al said, "and offered her a better way to get revenge on me."

"By setting your son up for a murder charge."

Big Al shrugged.

"Okay," Clint said, "she's the leader, right?"

"Yeah," Big Al said, "the other two are probably Tony Black and Andy Choate."

"They are."

"How do you know?"

"We talked to Choate's mother."

"We?"

"Me and the sheriff."

"And what did Mary say?"

"You know her?"

"At one time we were very close," Henry said. "Don't let the way she looks when she's at work fool you. She was a beautiful woman, and still can be. What'd she say?"

"That her son and Black were sweet on Stephanie."

"Most men are," Big Al said. "She's a formidable woman."

"Can she use that gun?"

"Very well."

"But she hasn't killed anyone?"

"Not that I know of."

"That's what I'm worried about," Clint said. "I prefer to know whether or not I'm dealing with someone experienced."

"Well," he said, "if she killed Ed Collins, then she's experienced."

"Not at facing a man with a gun."

THIRTY-SIX

Clint left Big Al's hotel and went back to his own. He went to his room, set a few booby traps at the door and windows to warn him if someone tried to get in. Only then did he take off his boots . . .

In another part of town, Andy Choate told Stephanie Kitten and Tony Black about Clint and the sheriff visiting his mother.

"What did she tell them?" Stephanie asked.

"You know Ma," Andy said. "She didn't tell them nothin'."

"I know your ma," Stephanie said. "She told them somethin'."

"She told them that you had me and Tony under your control," Andy said.

"What?" Tony asked.

"Well," Stephanie said with a grin, "she got that much right."

"So what do we do?" Andy asked. "Get out of town?"

"No," Stephanie said, "that's not an option. Thayer paid us to get rid of Adams. Once he's dead, the judge can try little Jason. And then my pa can rest easy."

"Will that satisfy you?" Tony asked.

"Maybe," Stephanie said. "Maybe not." She looked at her two friends. "We'll just have to wait and see."

Clint was starting to get sleepy when there was a knock on his door. He expected it to be Letty, but took his gun to the door anyway.

He cracked open the door, was surprised to see Mary Choate standing in the hall.

"Can I come in?" she asked.

"It's late . . ."

"Oh, don't be a fraidy cat," she said. "I'm not gonna hurt you."

Clint shrugged, opened the door, checked the hall as she slid past him. She smelled of her restaurant and of sweat—although Clint never minded the smell of a woman's own perspiration. Hers was earthy, and not sour at all.

She turned to face him as he closed the door. She was wearing a simple cotton dress, and while she was in her forties and had some thickening to her hips and waist, the dress molded itself to her and showed that she was still an extremely attractive woman with full breasts and a handsome face.

"Are you gonna shoot me?" she asked.

He didn't answer, but he walked to the bed post and holstered the gun.

"What can I do for you, Mrs. Choate?"

"Oh, no, no, dumpling, don't call me that," she said. "Just call me Mary."

"All right, Mary."

"I'm worried about my son," she said. "I'm thinkin' those two friends of his might get him killed. In fact, I'm worried you might kill him."

"That's not my goal, Mary," Clint said. "I'm going to do my best not to kill any of them."

"Oh, that girl," Mary said, "she'll make you kill her, or kill you. I don't know about Tony. I wouldn't have thought he had it in him, but under the influence of that girl, who knows?"

"So are you here to give me more information?"

"Not really," she said. "In fact, I'm not sure why I'm here. I'm thinkin' maybe I want you to take me to bed."

His jaw dropped. Suddenly he wondered what he would do if there was another knock on the door and it was Letty.

"Mary—"

"I know I'm Andy's mother, but I'm not too old," she said.

"I don't think you're too old at all—"

"Good," she said.

Much as Letty had done, Mary shucked her clothes, only it was easier for her. She was only wearing a dress. She seemed to shrug her shoulders, and the dress was on the floor.

He was right. She had full, round breasts with dark nipples, was a little thick in the waist and hips, but all that meant was that she was a woman, with a woman's body.

She came toward him and he annoyed himself by taking a step back.

"Mary—"

"Oh, dumpling," she said, "come on, you've done this

before. And it's been a while for me, so let's just do this. I know I probably should've taken a bath—"

"Never mind," he said, taking two steps forward to counteract the one step back, and reaching for her, "you don't need a bath . . ."

There was a lot of instruction during his time with Letty, but with Mary Choate, none of that was necessary. She was experienced, and knew what she liked.

She practically stripped Clint's clothes off and pushed him down on the bed. She attacked his hard cock, stroking it with both hands, then sucking it avidly until he almost exploded into her mouth—but she stopped him.

"Mmm, not yet, lamb chop," she said. "I'm not finished with you yet."

"Come up here," he said, pulling her up so that she was lying on top of him. He kissed her, and her tongue darted into his mouth. She slid up so that she was sitting with his cock trapped between them. She rubbed her pubic bush over him, and through it, he could feel how wet she was.

"Mmm, here I come, potpie," she said—and he didn't find her food endearments annoying at all. Not at that moment anyway.

She lifted her hips and then came down on him, engulfing her in the hot steaming depths of her pussy, and then started riding him.

Clint wasn't worried about Letty showing up anymore.

THIRTY-SEVEN

"Why don't we just go to his room," Tony Black suggested, "and kill him."

"Tonight?" Andy said. They were sitting in Scott's Saloon with a beer in front of each of them.

"Yeah, why not?" Tony asked. "Let's get it out of the way while we can."

"No," Stephanie said.

Both men looked at her.

"What?" Andy asked.

"No," she said, "we're not gonna sneak into his hotel and bushwhack him."

"Why not?" Tony asked.

"Because he deserves better than that," she said. "And I wanna kill him in the street, fair and square."

"That's crazy," Black said. "Andy, tell 'er she's crazy."

Andy looked from Tony to Stephanie and back again, wondering if he should speak up or keep quiet.

"Never mind, Andy," Stephanie said, saving him the trouble of deciding. "We're not doin' it that way."

"I ain't about to face the Gunsmith in the street, Steph," Tony said.

"You won't have to," Stephanie said. "I'll do that."

"Steph, that's crazy!" Tony said.

"Don't worry," she said, "I'll be in the street, but you boys will be there—somewhere."

"So . . . we *are* gonna bushwhack him?" Andy asked.

"We're gonna do what we have to do to get the job done," Stephanie said.

Tony Black sat back in his chair and heaved a sign of relief.

"You scared me," he said. "I thought you really meant to face him fair."

Stephanie reached out and ruffled Tony's hair. He was handsome, all right, but they had grown up together, and to her, he was more like a brother.

"I ain't totally crazy, Tony," she told him.

She looked at Andy, who seemed far away.

"What's wrong with you?"

"Ah," he said, "when my ma was talkin' to Adams and the sheriff, I got the feelin' . . . well, the way she was talkin' to him . . ."

"Your mom's a real slut, Andy," Stephanie said. "Are you thinkin' she wasn't gonna ride the Gunsmith's bronc?"

"Don't say that!"

"Hell," Tony said, laughing, "maybe she's up there right now, ridin' his—"

"I can't punch Steph, Tony, but I'll punch you if'n you don't stop talking about my mama like that."

"Hey," Tony said, "I'm not the one who said she's a slut."

"Ah," Andy said, "you two." He stood up and stormed out.

"Hey, come on, Andy," Stephanie said, "don't get mad!"

She and Tony laughed and drank their beer.

Clint had Mary on her knees and elbows, was fucking her ass from behind, which was the way she wanted it.

"Come on, come on," she was imploring him, "make me your whore, fuck me . . ."

He was slamming into her so hard it made ripples run through her butt cheeks. And each time he rammed his cock into her, she slammed her butt back against him, so that he was taking her as deeply as he could.

At one point Clint thought he heard someone knocking on his door, but he ignored it. His cock was much too deep inside Mary for him to withdraw and answer the door.

Finally, she flipped over—performing the maneuver without letting him go—and wrapped her legs around him while he continued fucking her. She drummed her heels on his ass, so that he was sure he was going to have a collection of bruises there.

Finally, he couldn't hold back any longer. He rammed himself deep, held it there, and grunted loudly as he emptied himself into her . . .

"That was great," she told him as she pulled her dress back on. "I ain't been fucked that good in a month of Sundays."

"Happy to oblige," Clint said, lying on his back in bed and catching his breath.

She came over and gave him a long, lingering kiss, also gripping his cock tightly for just a second.

"Don't get yourself killed, dumpling," she told him.

"What—"

But she was out the door and gone.

THIRTY-EIGHT

In the morning Clint decided to confront both Thayer and Judge Miller with what he had learned. He went to the sheriff's office to let the man know what he intended to do.

"I can't go with you," Brown said. "Not while I still want to keep my badge."

"I understand," Clint said. "You can't very well spit in the faces of your bosses."

"If and when we prove that one of them hired the killing done," Brown said, "I'll lock that man's ass in my jail. But before that—"

"Got it," Clint said.

"Let me know how it goes."

Clint left the sheriff's office, decided to talk to the judge before going to Daniel Thayer's house.

The judge's clerk told Clint that Miller was not in his office; he was in his courtroom.

"Is court in session?" Clint asked.

"No," the clerk said, "he just likes to spend time in there."

The clerk told Clint where the courtroom was. Clint found it, entered, and found Judge Miller sitting on his bench.

"I'll bet you like it up there," Clint said.

The judge stared down from behind the big desk, squinted, then said, "Is that you, Adams?"

"It's me."

"Come closer," Miller said.

Clint did, stopped when he got to where a prosecutor would be standing.

"I earned this position," Miller said, "so yes, I do enjoy sitting up here. What brings you here?"

"I was wondering how your jury selection was coming," Clint asked.

"If you're volunteering, I can't use you," Miller said. "I'm afraid you'd be somewhat biased."

"Not volunteering," Clint said, "just curious."

"I need a couple more jurors, and then we'll be set to try the Henry boy."

"Well," Clint said, "you might want to hold off on that."

"And why would I want to do that?" Judge Miller asked.

"I believe I know who the real killers are," Clint said, "and I'm just hours away from finding them."

"Is that so?"

"It is. And when I do, I can find out who hired them."

"And who might they be, these hired killers?"

Clint pretended to think about the question, then said, "Not going to tell you that right now."

"And why not?"

"Well, just in case they're working for you," Clint said, "I don't want you warning them."

Miller shook his head and said, "Gall."

"Just wanted you to know."

"Do you really think someone of my standing would stoop to hiring killers?"

"I don't know," Clint said, "would you?"

Miller hesitated, then leaned both elbows on the bench in front of him. "If I did," he said, "I'd hire good ones. See how that sits with you."

"Your honor," Clint said with a small bow, "permission to leave the court?"

Judge Miller simply gave Clint a dismissive wave.

Clint did not find Daniel Thayer in his little house. He knocked, walked around the house, and looked inside, but no one was there.

He went back to town to Milty's, where Randy was taking chairs down from the tables, getting ready for the day.

"Coffee or beer?" he asked.

"Coffee," Clint said. "Reminds me that I haven't had breakfast yet."

"Have a seat," Randy said. "I was just about to have mine. I'll bring some extra out."

"Thanks."

Randy went to the back of the saloon, apparently to the kitchen. He came out with a tray with a coffeepot and two mugs, then went back and returned with two plates of eggs, bacon, and spuds, along with some biscuits.

"My God," Clint said, "these eggs are like clouds. Who's your cook?"

Randy sat across from him and said, "I cook it myself."

"Jeez," Clint said, biting into a fluffy biscuit, "why don't you serve food?"

"Naw," Randy said, "I just cook for myself. I'm really just a bartender."

"This is the best food I've had since I got to town," Clint said.

"Thanks," Randy said, "but I like cookin' for myself and Letty."

"Speaking of Letty, I haven't see her in a while."

"Me neither," Randy said, "and the last time I saw her, I didn't recognize her. She was . . . clean."

"Is that unusual?"

"It sure is," Randy said. "It might be a man."

"Would that be bad?"

"For him," Randy said. "If I find out who it is, I'll make him a gelding."

Clint kept quiet.

"So what brings you by so early?"

"You got any idea where I can find Daniel Thayer?"

"His house, I imagine."

"I checked there," Clint said.

"The big house?"

"What big house?"

"Ah," Randy said, "you went to that little house he has. He likes people to think he lives modestly."

"And he doesn't?"

"Hell, no. He's got a huge house about a mile outside of town. Had it built special. But when he's in town, he stays in that little house. Fools people—some people—into thinking he's not, well, full of himself . . . which he is."

"So how do I get to that house?"

"Easy," Randy said, "just ride out the main road . . ." He gave Clint some simple directions.

"Okay, I'll get out there and talk to him, let him know I'm in on his little secret."

"When will you do that?"

Clint stuffed some eggs into his mouth and said, "As soon as I finish eating."

THIRTY-NINE

This time when Clint knocked on Thayer's door, it was opened by a white-haired man in a suit.

"Yes, sir?"

"Clint Adams to see Mr. Thayer."

"Do you have an appointment?"

"A standing invitation."

"Come in, then."

The man let him in and closed the door. Randy was right—this house was enormous, with four large columns on the outside, a huge entry foyer on the inside.

"Wait here."

Clint waited while the man went down a hallway.

Hollis was a combination butler and man Friday to Daniel Thayer.

He walked down the hall to his master's study. Thayer was seated there in a silk dressing down, drinking tea.

"Yes?"

"A Mr. Clint Adams is here to see you, sir."

"Here? At the house?"

"Yes, sir. He says he has a standing invitation."

Thayer thought a moment. Had Adams caught Stephanie and her idiots? Was the Gunsmith here for him now? He couldn't hope to match Adams with a gun. He was going to have to try to bluff.

"Take him to the big living room, Hollis," Thayer said. "I will join him there."

"Yes, sir."

Thayer left the study to go to his bedroom and get dressed.

Hollis found Clint loitering in the foyer and said, "Come with me, sir."

"Lead on."

Hollis led Clint to a large living room. The furniture was more expensive than anything he'd ever seen in any hotel. This house, the furniture—he was starting to think that maybe Thayer *was* richer than Big Al Henry.

"Mr. Thayer will join you shortly."

"Thanks."

Hollis withdrew. Clint wondered if Thayer would appear with a gun, or with help. Maybe Stephanie and her friends? He had to stay ready.

Ten minutes later Daniel Thayer appeared, dressed in a gray suit, both hands empty. Clint looked behind him, but he was alone.

"You won't need your gun, Mr. Adams," Thayer said, reading Clint's body language. "I'm not armed."

"Anyone else in the house?"

"Just Hollis," Thayer said. "Can I offer you a brandy?"

"I know who the killers are, Thayer," Clint said. "When I catch them, they'll tell me who hired them."

Thayer walked to a sideboard and poured himself a brandy. He turned to face Clint with the glass in his hand.

"That's good, isn't?"

"Yes," Clint said, "it is, if you didn't hire them."

Thayer sipped his brandy and said, "I didn't."

"Then the judge did."

"Maybe."

"One of you did," Clint said. "I'll find out which one."

"Well," Thayer said, "when you do, let me know."

"Count on it."

Clint turned to leave.

"Wait."

Clint turned.

"If you know who the killers are, tell me."

"Oh, I will," Clint promised. "After I find them."

He left the living room and the house.

Hollis came back in, found Thayer still standing there, sipping his brandy.

"Everything all right, sir?"

"No," Thayer said. "No, Hollis, everything is most assuredly not all right."

"Well," Hollis said, "you will fix it, sir. You always do."

"I'll need you to deliver a message."

Hollis nodded.

Thayer wondered if he could throw money at the problem and fix it this time.

FORTY

Clint rode Eclipse back to town from Daniel Thayer's house. This was the first time since he'd arrived in Copper Canyon that he needed the big Darley. After checking Eclipse over, Clint was satisfied that the horse had been well taken care of.

He rode back to the livery, gave the horse back to the hostler.

"You're taking good care of him," he told the man.

"Thanks. I—"

"Keep it up," Clint said.

The hostler, an older man who had spent a lifetime handling horses, blinked and said, "Course I will. This is the greatest horse I've ever seen."

"Yes, he is," Clint said.

He left the livery, walked to the sheriff's office.

"Back already?" Brown asked.

"I spoke to both the judge and Thayer—went out to Thayer's big house, which I didn't know he had."

"Don't tell me he fooled you with that small one."

"He did."

"Well, now you know."

"How rich is he anyway?"

"Nobody knows."

"Richer than Big Al?"

"Not according to Big Al."

"Okay," Clint said, sitting in the chair across from Brown, "how do we find Stephanie and her friends?"

Brown shrugged. "Watch Mary Choate's café."

"Could take too long."

"Okay then," Brown said, "one of us can watch her place, while the other one looks for them."

"You have no idea where they live?"

"No," the lawman said. "I mean, I thought Andy lived with his mother."

"Maybe he lives with Stephanie, or Tony."

"And maybe they all live together," Brown said. "Stephanie and Tony grew up together. They're almost sister and brother."

"And nobody has any idea where they're living now?" Clint asked.

"Well," Brown said, "I don't. Maybe the man who hired them does, though."

"And he—the judge or Thayer—is not about to tell us."

"I know!"

They both turned their heads toward the cell block door, where the voice had come from. They got up and walked over to it.

"What did you say?" Clint asked Jason.

The boy was standing at the door of his cell. He'd obviously been listening to their conversation.

"I said, I know where Stephanie Kitten lives."

"And how do you know that?" the sheriff asked.

"Well . . . she's very pretty," he said. "One day I was out walking and I saw her. I . . . followed her."

"Right to where she lives?" Clint asked.

"Yes."

"And you can tell me how to get there?"

Jason frowned.

"I don't know if I can tell you . . ." Then he brightened. "But I can show you."

Clint looked at Brown.

"Oh, no," Brown said. "You want me to let him out of his cell?"

"It's the only way."

"Why do you believe him?"

"Sheriff," Clint said, "aren't we pretty sure he didn't kill Ed Collins?"

"Yes, but it's not up to me to make those decisions."

"I'm not asking you to let him go," Clint said, "just let him come with me, and show me where they live. Then I'll bring him right back."

"And what if he decides to escape?"

"Jason," Clint said, "if I let you out, and you try to run, that would be bad, right?"

"Yes, sir."

"And you don't want to be bad, right?"

"No, sir."

"Your father would be very disappointed in you."

"Yes, sir, he would."

"So after you help me find where Stephanie lives, you'll come right back here with me, won't you?"

"Yes, sir, I will."

Clint looked at the lawman.

"There you go."

"And I'm just supposed to take his word for it?"

"No," Clint said, "take mine. I'll bring him back."

Brown thought about it.

"Sheriff, you go and watch the café," Clint said. "If they show up there, you can follow them. Don't brace them. Wait for me."

"And?"

"And if I find out where they live, I'll come and get you," Clint said. "And bring Jason back here at the same time."

"If the judge finds out—"

"If he hired them, it won't matter," Clint said. "And even if he didn't, and we prove Jason's innocent, then we'll have saved him from prosecuting an innocent boy. He may want Jason to be guilty, but he won't frame him."

"He won't?"

"No," Clint said, "he likes being a judge too much."

Brown ran his hand over his head, rubbed his hair a few times vigorously.

"I don't know about this."

"I do," Clint said. "Come on, Sheriff. Take a chance."

Brown gave it some more thought, then reluctantly took the cell key from the wall peg and handed it to Clint.

"Go ahead."

FORTY-ONE

"Can I go see my father?" Jason asked when they were outside the jailhouse.

"Not just yet," Clint said.

"But—"

"We have a job to do, Jason," Clint said. "We have to find Stephanie and her friends."

"But why?"

"Because I think—I'm sure they killed Mr. Collins."

"But why?"

"I can't explain it to you now," Clint said. "Do we need horses to find them?"

"No," the boy said, "no, we can walk."

"Okay, then," Clint said. "Lead the way, Jason."

Jason started to walk, then stopped and asked, "Am I a deputy now?"

"No, Jason."

"Are you?"

"No," Clint said, "neither of us are deputies. We're just helping the sheriff with his job."

"Ain't that what a deputy does?"

"Yes, it is."

"Do you think the sheriff will make me a deputy after this?"

"Jason," Clint said, "before you can even ask him, we have to prove that you're innocent. And we can't do that until we find Stephanie. Understand?"

"I understand."

"Then let's go."

The boy nodded, and started walking.

"Wait," Clint said.

"What?" Jason turned.

"My hotel first."

"Why?'

"I have to get something."

They changed directions.

Sheriff Gordon Brown walked to Mary Choate's café, took a quick look inside through the window. He did not spot Stephanie Kitten, Tony Black, or Andy Choate. Mary was bustling about in her apron, serving her customers.

Brown walked across the street and took up position in the doorway of an abandoned store. He folded his arms across his chest and settled down to wait.

Jason Henry led Clint outside of town in a direction Clint had not yet gone. Up ahead it looked like heavy brush.

"Jason, are you sure you're heading in the right direction?" he asked.

"We have to go through those bushes," he said.

It only occurred to Clint that the boy might be leading him into a trap because of past experience. It had served him well over the years to suspect everyone. However, he was fairly certain that this boy was exactly what he appeared to be—innocent, and simpleminded.

Jason pushed through the brush and Clint followed.

In their house, Stephanie Kitten sat across from Tom and Andy and said, "I've decided to let Clint Adams come to us."

"What makes you think he'll do that?"

"I got word from Thayer that Adams was at his house, saying he knew who the killers were."

"Did he mention us by name?" Andy asked.

"No."

"Then what makes you think he knows it's us?" Andy asked.

"Or that he'll find us?" Tony added.

"The boy," Stephanie said.

"Jason?" Andy asked.

"He knows where we live."

"How? Nobody knows about this house. It was abandoned years ago. Nobody knows we found it and fixed it up."

"He does," she said.

"How?" Andy asked.

"He followed me here once."

"What? And you didn't tell us?"

"I thought he was just a sweet, simpleminded boy with a crush," she said. "I didn't think he'd tell anybody."

"And now you do?" Tony asked.

"This is a different situation," she said. "I'm sure Adams will explore every possibility to find us."

"Like questioning the boy?" Tony asked.

"Yes."

"Damn it," Andy said, looking around. "You mean they might be on their way here right now?"

"If Thayer was right," she said, "yes. He was headed back to town to find us."

"If he brings the law—" Tony started.

"The judge will take care of that."

"What makes you think so?"

"Because Thayer will see to it," she told him. "And the judge wants to put that boy on trial."

"If that kid comes here," Tony said, "I'll kill him."

"That wouldn't be a good idea, Tony," she said. "We still need him to take the fall."

"This sounds to me like everything is fallin' apart," Andy said.

"Don't you fall apart on me now, Andy. I need you." She reached out and stroked his hair.

"Yeah, Steph," he said, leaning into her touch. "Okay."

"Tony?" she said. "Can I count on you?"

"You know you can always count on me, Steph."

"Then let's get into position before Clint Adams gets here," she told them.

"And what if he doesn't show up?"

"He's gonna find us, Andy," she said. "We just have to make sure that when he does, we make him sorry."

FORTY-TWO

"There," Jason said, pointing.

Clint saw the house. It was in bad shape, even though it was obvious somebody had tried to fix it up.

"I can go to the door and knock—"

"No," Clint said, keeping his voice down. "You stay right here and don't move. Understand?"

"I understand."

Clint looked around. It was quiet . . . too quiet.

"I'm going to circle around to the back," he told Jason. "Stay right here like I told you, Jason. Don't move."

"I won't."

Clint hoped Jason was telling the truth. And if he was, he hoped the boy would not be tempted to move.

Or run.

He circled around to come at the house from the back. The work that had been done to shore up the house was more evident from the rear. It was amateurish, but effective.

He didn't rush, and hoped Jason would stay patient.

* * *

As soon as Clint left Jason alone, the boy became frightened. He looked around him, as if he expected someone to come after him. He was out of jail, and he wanted desperately to stay out. The only person he thought could help him to do that would be his father.

He had promised Clint Adams that he wouldn't move, and wouldn't run, but he couldn't keep that promise. He had to get to his father.

He turned to run, but ran right into someone.

Clint waited.

What if Stephanie Kitten was as smart as she was pretty? What if Thayer had told her and her boys to get rid of him? How would they go about it? Call him out? Not likely? Bushwhack him? Much more likely.

He wondered if Thayer had had time to warn them since he'd seen him this morning. If so, they had either cleared out, or were waiting for him.

At that point Clint saw some movement through a window. A figure with long blond hair. If the girl was inside alone . . .

"Stephanie!" he shouted. "Stephanie Kitten!"

There was no answer, but her face appeared in the back window.

"Stephanie!"

Her face disappeared and then the back door opened. She stood in the doorway—hip cocked against the doorjamb—as if she was totally unconcerned.

"Who are you?" she asked. "Why are you yelling my name?"

"My name is Clint Adams."

She cocked her hip the other way, still posing. She was undeniably a beautiful woman. She also folded her arms beneath her full breasts, for good measure.

"So then, why is the Gunsmith calling out my name?"

"I want to talk."

"So come in and talk," she said. "Why didn't you just knock on the door, like a civilized gentleman?"

"I wasn't sure of the kind of reception I'd get," he told her.

"Come on in and I'll show you," she said. "I've got some good whiskey."

She didn't wait for an answer. She left the doorway, but the door remained open.

Clint looked around, moved cautiously from his position. No one with guns jumped out at him. He closed the distance to the house, entered, and closed the door behind him. He found himself in a small kitchen with a very old stove, a table with three good legs and one repaired one, and matching chairs.

"In here," her voice called.

He went to the kitchen doorway, saw Stephanie sitting on a worn sofa in a sparely furnished living room.

"I'm sorry," she said, "the place needs a cleaning."

Sitting in the midst of near squalor, she appeared even more beautiful. Her hair seemed to shimmer, and he could smell the Rosebud soap on her. He now knew he was right.

"Well," she said, "Clint Adams." She leaned her elbow on the back of the sofa, rested her cocked head on her hand. She knew all the fetching poses. "What can I do for you?"

"You can tell me who hired you to kill Ed Collins," Clint said.

"What?"

"And why you decided to frame poor Jason Henry for it."

She dropped her arm and said, "Are you serious?"

"Very," he said. "See, I think Daniel Thayer hired you and your two boyfriends for the job. I just need you to confirm that."

"I can't confirm somethin' that didn't happen," she said.

"Meaning you didn't kill him," Clint asked, "or Thayer didn't hire you to do it?"

"Both," she said, then frowned and added, "or neither. Which is it?"

"Both," Clint said. "By the way, where are your two boyfriends?"

"They're not my boyfriends," she said, "they're my . . . partners."

"Partners in what?" Clint asked. "Crime? Murder?"

"Business."

Clint laughed.

"What business have you three been involved in?"

"That's none of *your* business," she said. "Anything else?"

He studied her. She was calm, and she wasn't going to break. One of her partners might be easier.

"Where are your boys?"

She shrugged.

"Are you sure they're not waiting for me outside?"

"What for?"

"To bushwhack me?"

She stood up.

"If I wanted to kill you, I'd do it myself."

"You think you can?" he asked. "You fancy yourself good with that gun? Have you ever killed a man face-to-face, Stephanie? Not like you killed Ed Collins, with two partners to help, but alone. Face-to-face. On even terms?"

She didn't answer him, but he saw a muscle jumping uncontrollably in her jaw.

He laughed.

"They are outside, aren't they?" he asked. "You were expecting me. Thayer told you I saw him today, and you expected me to find you here. You're good, Stephanie." She was good at handling men, but was she good at handling a gun?

"Come on," he said.

"What?"

"Let's leave them out there waiting," he said. "Let's do this, you and me."

"Right now?"

"Sure," he said. "Why wait? Anybody who thinks they're good with a gun, like you, is always dying to test themselves against somebody like me."

He stared right into her eyes, saw a flicker there. Doubt? Or fear?

"Come on, Stephanie," Clint said. "Go for your gun."

FORTY-THREE

"No."

"No?" he asked. "Why not?"

"There's nobody around to see," she said. "If I kill you, I want witnesses."

"You mean an audience?" he asked. "You youngsters, you're all the same. You need that audience."

"If I kill the Gunsmith, I want people to see it."

"Hmm," he said. "So you're not scared."

"Not in the least."

"Okay," he said. "If I go outside and your boys are there, I'm going to kill them both."

She didn't answer.

"You don't care, do you?"

"If they're stupid enough to go up against you, they deserve to get killed."

"Wow," Clint said, "if only they knew how little you think of them."

"Please," she said. "They're little boys. I need a man."

"Like Thayer?"

"Him?" she asked. "He's not a man. In fact, I've never met a real man." She stared at him, and then her face changed, as if something occurred to her. "Wait, maybe you . . ."

She came toward him, the sweet smell of her soap moving ahead of her.

"That scent . . ."

"Yes?" Her hands went to the buttons of her shirt and she started to undo them.

"Jason smelled it in the store . . ."

"What?"

"When you killed Ed Collins."

She had the shirt mostly open, her full breasts and pale skin showing, then she stopped.

"Do you really want to talk about that now?" she asked, running the fingertips of her left hand over the skin of the right breast. He figured she was hoping he'd watch that hand, but he had his eyes on her right, hovering over her gun.

"Do it, Stephanie," he said in a low tone.

"What?"

"Skin that hog-leg," he said. "Come on."

She pulled her right hand away from her gun as if it were hot, started buttoning the shirt again. She turned her back to him.

"Get out."

"I told you—"

"I know what you told me," she said. "Just get out."

"Okay," he said. "It's your call."

Instead of going out the back door, he walked to the front, opened it, and stepped out.

FORTY-FOUR

The first shot went high and wild.

Clint didn't move. He couldn't show any fear, or concern.

"Wow," he called, "which of you fired that shot? That was way off. You must've rushed it."

No answer.

"Come on, boys, step out," he said. "Let's do this."

Tony Black stepped out of hiding. He was off to Clint's right.

"Where's Andy, Tony?"

"Here!"

He looked to his left. Andy stepped out, but he wasn't alone. He had Jason right in front of him.

Damn.

Clint stepped away from the house. He heard Stephanie come out the front door, so he moved farther away. Now he was out in the open, the center of a triangle formed by the other three.

Okay, this was the situation he's foreseen himself getting into—but not with Jason in the play.

"Okay," Stephanie said to him, "you wanted me to go for my gun. Let's do it."

"Sure," he said, "now that you've got your boys backing you up."

"What's the difference?" she asked. "You're the big man, the Gunsmith. This can't be new to you."

"Oh, it's not," Clint said. "You're right, I've been through this many times before, and I'm still alive." He looked over at her two partners. "You boys really want to die so your girlfriend can make a reputation for herself?"

"Shut up!" Tony Black said.

Clint ignored him, looked at Stephanie.

"This is bad, Steph," he said. "You're going to die."

"There's three of us, and one of you," she said. "And that brain-addled boy is in the way. He's gonna die."

"If he dies, you die," Clint said.

"You can't get all of us," she said. "We're spread out way too far."

"I can get you, though," he said. "You're the first one I'll kill."

"You been outsmarted, Gunsmith," Tony shouted. "Stephanie's too smart."

"She's the smartest," Andy chimed in.

"Clint?" Jason said. Andy had his left arm around the boy's chest.

"Just stand still, Jason," Clint said. "No matter what happens. Okay?" If the boy moved at the wrong time, he might walk right into a bullet.

"A-All right."

"Now the rest of you," Clint said. "You've got one last chance."

"The last chance was yours," Stephanie said, "and you're out of time . . ."

She went for her gun.

Tony Black was nervous. His hands were sweating, and he had his eyes on Stephanie. As soon as she went for her gun, that was his signal.

He saw her move, and he grabbed for his with his sweaty palm.

Andy was watching both the Gunsmith and Stephanie. She had told him not to go for his gun until she went for hers, but he kept thinking, What if Adams draws first?

In the end it was Stephanie who went first, but Adams had his guns out, and Andy never saw him move.

Guns?

Clint drew his .45 Colt from his holster with his right hand, and the .32 New Line from behind his back with his left. He'd intended to shoot Stephanie with his modified Colt, and either Black or Choate with the New Line, but they were too far away for him to use the .32. The caliber was too small, and one shot might not take them down.

So he crossed his arms at the last moment, shot her with the .32 and Tony Black with the .45.

One shot each. The .45 slug hit Tony in the chest, exploded his heart, and killed him instantly.

The .32 hit Stephanie right between her beautiful eyes. Her head snapped back and she slumped to the ground.

He turned to face Andy, both guns pointed.

Andy panicked, drew his gun, and tightened his hold on Jason. He hid behind the boy as fully as he could, pointing his gun at Clint.

He was scared.

Clint knew Andy was scared, which meant he might do anything.

"Take it easy, Andy."

"You—you killed 'em both."

"Yes, I did."

"I—I never saw you draw."

"Andy," Clint said, "I promised your mother I'd try not to kill you. I hope you'll help me keep that promise."

"I'll kill the boy," Andy said. "I'll kill Jason if—if—" Andy didn't know what to ask for.

"Andy," Clint said, "you can walk away from this alive. But if you kill the boy, I'll have to kill you. You won't be leaving me any choice."

Andy wet his lips.

"If I let him go, you won't kill me?"

"Let him go, and drop your gun."

"A-And you'll let me go?"

"I can't do that," Clint said, "but you'll be alive for us to walk back to town together."

Andy's arms were getting tired, so tired.

"Andy?"

The boy dropped his gun to the ground, and his arm from around Jason's chest . . .

FORTY-FIVE

The next day Clint rode Eclipse to the front of Big Al Henry's hotel and dismounted. He went inside, found Henry waiting for him at his table.

"Good morning," Big Al said, putting an envelope on the table across from him.

Clint pulled out a chair and sat down in front of the envelope.

"I thought cash would be appropriate," Big Al said.

"Cash is fine."

A waiter came and poured some coffee for Clint.

"Thank you."

"Will you be ordering, sir?"

"Sure," Clint said. "Steak and eggs."

"Comin' up, sir."

"I have to thank you, Mr. Adams," Big Al said. "That boy, Andy? He exonerated my boy, implicated the woman and man you killed . . . and Daniel Thayer."

"That's good."

"The sheriff dropped the charges against my boy."

"How does the judge feel about that?" Clint asked.

"Not good," Henry said. "In fact, he's livid. But at least he wasn't caught prosecuting an innocent man."

"He can send me his thanks to General Delivery, Labyrinth, Texas."

"I'll tell him," Henry said. "When are you leaving town?"

"Right after breakfast."

"Say good-bye to everybody you had to say good-bye to?"

"No," he said. He still hadn't seen Letty. He suspected she had come to his room while he was with Mary, and heard them. Maybe she even knocked, and he hadn't heard. At least she hadn't seemed to tell her uncle what had transpired between them.

As for Mary Choate, she was very grateful that he had not killed her son. But then, he had also put Andy in jail, so there was no good-bye there.

"Are you interested in what happened with Beth Collins?" Henry asked.

"Huh? What happened?"

"I bought her father's store," he said. "Gave her a good price."

"That's nice."

"I'm going to let Jason run it."

"Is that wise?"

"I'll also have somebody experienced in there with him, to show him the ropes," Big Al said. "He'll be fine."

"I hope so."

"Where do you go from here?"

"I don't know, actually," Clint said. "I'm just going to ride. Try to stay out of trouble."

"I imagine that's hard for you."

Clint looked up at the waiter as he set his breakfast down in front of him and said, "You have no idea."

Watch for

SHOWDOWN IN DESPERATION

391st novel in the exciting GUNSMITH series
from Jove

Coming in July!

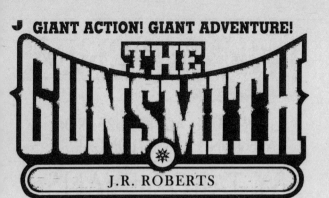

GIANT ACTION! GIANT ADVENTURE!

THE GUNSMITH

J.R. ROBERTS

penguin.com/actionwesterns

M455AS0812

GIANT-SIZED ADVENTURE FROM AVENGING ANGEL LONGARM.

BY TABOR EVANS

penguin.com/actionwesterns

M456AS0812

DON'T MISS A YEAR OF

Slocum Giant
by
Jake Logan

Slocum Giant 2004:
Slocum in the Secret
Service

Slocum Giant 2005:
Slocum and the Larcenous
Lady

Slocum Giant 2006:
Slocum and the Hanging
Horse

Slocum Giant 2007:
Slocum and the Celestial
Bones

Slocum Giant 2008:
Slocum and the Town
Killers

Slocum Giant 2009:
Slocum's Great
Race

Slocum Giant 2010:
Slocum Along
Rotten Row

Slocum Giant 2013:
Slocum and the Silver
City Harlot

penguin.com/actionwesterns

M457AS0812

Jove Westerns put the "wild" back into the Wild West

LONGARM
by Tabor Evans

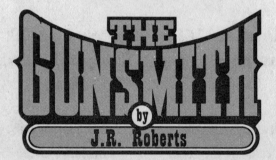

THE GUNSMITH
by
J.R. Roberts

SLOCUM by
JAKE LOGAN

Don't miss these exciting, all-action series!
penguin.com/actionwesterns

M11G0610